The Fitz-Boodle Papers by William Makepeace Thackeray

The great author of Vanity Fair and The Luck Of Barry Lyndon was born in India in 1811.

At age 5 his father died and his mother sent him back to England. His education was of the best but he himself seemed unable to apply his talents to a rigorous work ethic.

However, once he harnessed his talents the works flowed in novels, articles, short stories, sketches and lectures.

Sadly, his personal life was rather more difficult. After a few years of marriage his wife began to suffer from depression and over the years became detached from reality. Thackeray himself suffered from ill health later in his life and the one pursuit that kept him moving forward was that of writing. In his life time, he was placed second only to Dickens. High praise indeed.

Index of Contents

PREFACE

GEORGE FITZ-BOODLE, ESQUIRE, TO OLIVER YORKE, ESQUIRE.

OMNIUM CLUB, May 20, 1842.

DEAR SIR,—I have always been considered the third-best whist-player in Europe, and (though never betting more than five pounds) have for many years past added considerably to my yearly income by my skill in the game, until the commencement of the present season, when a French gentleman, Monsieur Lalouette, was admitted to the club where I usually play. His skill and reputation were so great, that no men of the club were inclined to play against us two of a side; and the consequence has been, that we have been in a manner pitted against one another. By a strange turn of luck (for I cannot admit the idea of his superiority), Fortune, since the Frenchman's arrival, has been almost constantly against me, and I have lost two-and-thirty nights in the course of a couple of score of nights' play.

Everybody knows that I am a poor man; and so much has Lalouette's luck drained my finances, that only last week I was obliged to give him that famous gray cob on which you have seen me riding in the Park (I can't afford a thoroughbred, and hate a cocktail),—I was, I say, forced to give him up my cob in exchange for four ponies which I owed him. Thus, as I never walk, being a heavy man whom nobody cares to mount, my time hangs heavily on my hands; and, as I hate home, or that apology for it—a bachelor's lodgings—and as I have nothing earthly to do now until I can afford to purchase another horse, I spend my time in sauntering from one club to another, passing many rather listless hours in them before the men come in.

You will say, Why not take to backgammon, or ecarte, or amuse yourself with a book? Sir (putting out of the question the fact that I do not play upon credit), I make a point never to play before candles are lighted; and as for books, I must candidly confess to you I am not a reading man.

'Twas but the other day that some one recommended me to your Magazine after dinner, saying it contained an exceedingly witty article upon—I forget what. I give you my honor, sir, that I took up the work at six, meaning to amuse myself till seven, when Lord Trumpington's dinner was to come off, and egad! in two minutes I fell asleep, and never woke till midnight. Nobody ever thought of looking for me in the library, where nobody ever goes; and so ravenously hungry was I, that I was obliged to walk off to Crockford's for supper.

What is it that makes you literary persons so stupid? I have met various individuals in society who I was told were writers of books, and that sort of thing, and expecting rather to be amused by their conversation, have invariably found them dull to a degree, and as for information, without a particle of it. Sir, I actually asked one of these fellows, "What was the nick to seven?" and he stared in my face and said he didn't know. He was hugely over-dressed in satin, rings, chains and so forth; and at the beginning of dinner was disposed to be rather talkative and pert; but my little sally silenced HIM, I promise you, and got up a good laugh at his expense too. "Leave George alone," said little Lord Cinqbars, "I warrant he'll be a match for any of you literary fellows." Cinqbars is no great wiseacre; but, indeed, it requires no great wiseacre to know THAT.

What is the simple deduction to be drawn from this truth? Why, this—that a man to be amusing and well-informed, has no need of books at all, and had much better go to the world and to men for his knowledge. There was Ulysses, now, the Greek fellow engaged in the Trojan war, as I dare say you know; well, he was the cleverest man possible, and how? From having seen men and cities, their manners noted and their realms surveyed, to be sure. So have I. I have been in every capital, and can order a dinner in every language in Europe.

My notion, then, is this. I have a great deal of spare time on my hands, and as I am told you pay a handsome sum to persons writing for you, I will furnish you occasionally with some of my views upon men and things; occasional histories of my acquaintance, which I think may amuse you; personal narratives of my own; essays, and what not. I am told that I do not spell correctly. This of course I don't know; but you will remember that Richelieu and Marlborough could not spell, and egad! I am an honest man, and desire to be no better than they. I know that it is the matter, and not the manner, which is of importance. Have the goodness, then, to let one of your understrappers correct the spelling and the grammar of my papers; and you can give him a few shillings in my name for his trouble.

Begging you to accept the assurance of my high consideration, I am, sir,

Your obedient servant,
GEORGE SAVAGE FITZ-BOODLE.

P.S.—By the way, I have said in my letter that I found ALL literary persons vulgar and dull. Permit me to contradict this with regard to yourself. I met you once at Blackwall, I think it was, and really did not remark anything offensive in your accent or appearance.

Before commencing the series of moral disquisitions, &c. which I intend, the reader may as well know who I am, and what my past course of life has been. To say that I am a Fitz-Boodle is to say at once that I am a gentleman. Our family has held the estate of Boodle ever since the reign of Henry II.; and it is out of no ill will to my elder brother, or unnatural desire for his death, but only because the estate is a very good one, that I wish heartily it was mine: I would say as much of Chatsworth or Eaton Hall.

I am not, in the first place, what is called a ladies' man, having contracted an irrepressible habit of smoking after dinner, which has obliged me to give up a great deal of the dear creatures' society; nor can I go much to country-houses for the same reason. Say what they will, ladies do not like you to smoke in their bedrooms: their silly little noses scent out the odor upon the chintz, weeks after you have left them. Sir John has been caught coming to bed particularly merry and redolent of cigar-smoke; young George, from Eton, was absolutely found in the little green-house puffing an Havana; and when discovered they both lay the blame upon Fitz-Boodle. "It was Mr. Fitz-Boodle, mamma," says George, "who offered me the cigar, and I did not like to refuse him." "That rascal Fitz seduced us, my dear," says Sir John, "and kept us laughing until past midnight." Her ladyship instantly sets me down as a person to be avoided. "George," whispers she to her boy, "promise me on your honor, when you go to town, not to know that man." And when she enters the breakfast-room for prayers, the first greeting is a peculiar expression of countenance, and inhaling of breath, by which my lady indicates the presence of some exceedingly disagreeable odor in the room. She makes you the faintest of curtsies, and regards you, if not with a "flashing eye," as in the novels, at least with a "distended nostril." During the whole of the service, her heart is filled with the blackest gall towards you; and she is thinking about the best means of getting you out of the house.

What is this smoking that it should be considered a crime? I believe in my heart that women are jealous of it, as of a rival. They speak of it as of some secret, awful vice that seizes upon a man, and makes him a pariah from genteel society. I would lay a guinea that many a lady who has just been kind enough to rend the above lines lays down the book, after this confession of mine that I am a smoker, and says, "Oh, the vulgar wretch!" and passes on to something else.

The fact is, that the cigar IS a rival to the ladies, and their conqueror too. In the chief pipe-smoking nations they are kept in subjection. While the chief, Little White Belt, smokes, the women are silent in his wigwam; while Mahomet Ben Jawbrahim causes volumes of odorous incense of Latakia to play round his beard, the women of the harem do not disturb his meditations, but only add to the delight of them by tinkling on a dulcimer and dancing before him. When Professor Strumpff of Gottingen takes down No. 13 from the wall, with a picture of Beatrice Cenci upon it, and which holds a pound of canaster, the Frau Professorin knows that for two hours Hermann is engaged, and takes up her stockings and knits in quiet. The constitution of French society has been quite changed within the last twelve years: an ancient and respectable dynasty has been overthrown; an aristocracy which Napoleon could never master has disappeared: and from what cause? I do not hesitate to say,—FROM THE HABIT OF SMOKING. Ask any man whether, five years before the revolution of July, if you wanted a cigar at Paris, they did not bring you a roll of tobacco with a straw in it! Now, the whole city smokes; society is changed; and be sure of this, ladies, a similar combat is going on in this country at present between cigar-smoking and you. Do you suppose you will conquer? Look over the wide world, and see that your adversary has overcome it. Germany has been puffing for threescore years; France smokes to a man. Do you think you can keep the enemy out of England? Psha! look at his progress. Ask the clubhouses, Have they smoking-rooms or not? Are they not obliged to yield to the general want of the age, in spite of the resistance of the old women on the committees? I, for my part, do not despair to see a bishop lolling out of the "Athenaeum" with a cheroot in his mouth, or, at any rate, a pipe stuck in his shovel-hat.

But as in all great causes and in promulgating new and illustrious theories, their first propounders and exponents are generally the victims of their enthusiasm, of course the first preachers of smoking have been martyrs, too; and George Fitz-Boodle is one. The first gas-man was ruined; the inventor of steam-engine printing became a pauper. I began to smoke in days when the task was one of some danger, and paid the penalty of my crime. I was flogged most fiercely for my first cigar; for, being asked to dine one Sunday evening with a half-pay colonel of dragoons (the gallant, simple, humorous Shortcut—heaven bless him!—I have had many a guinea from him who had so few), he insisted upon my smoking in his room at the "Salopian," and the consequence was, that I became so violently ill as to be reported intoxicated upon my return to Slaughter-House School, where I was a boarder, and I was whipped the next morning for my peccadillo. At Christ Church, one of our tutors was the celebrated lamented Otto Rose, who would have been a bishop under the present Government, had not an immoderate indulgence in water-gruel cut short his elegant and useful career. He was a good man, a pretty scholar and poet (the episode upon the discovery of eau-de-Cologne, in his prize-poem on "The Rhine," was considered a masterpiece of art, though I am not much of a judge myself upon such matters), and he was as remarkable for his fondness for a tuft as for his nervous antipathy to tobacco. As ill-luck would have it, my rooms (in Tom Quad) were exactly under his; and I was grown by this time to be a confirmed smoker. I was a baronet's son (we are of James the First's creation), and I do believe our tutor could have pardoned any crime in the world but this. He had seen me in a tandem, and at that moment was seized with a violent fit of sneezing—(sternutatory paroxysm he called it)—at the conclusion of which I was a mile down the Woodstock Road. He had seen me in pink, as we used to call it, swaggering in the open sunshine across a grass-plat in the court; but spied out opportunely a servitor, one Todhunter by name, who was going to morning chapel with his shoestring untied, and forthwith sprung towards that unfortunate person, to set him an imposition. Everything, in fact, but tobacco he could forgive. Why did cursed fortune bring him into the rooms over mine? The odor of the cigars made his gentle spirit quite furious; and one luckless morning, when I was standing before my "oak," and chanced to puff a great bouffee of Varinas into his face, he forgot his respect for my family altogether (I was the second son, and my brother a sickly creature THEN,—he is now sixteen stone in weight, and has a half-score of children); gave me a severe lecture, to which I replied rather hotly, as was my wont. And then came demand for an apology; refusal on my part; appeal to the dean; convocation; and rustication of George Savage Fitz-Boodle.

My father had taken a second wife (of the noble house of Flintskinner), and Lady Fitz-Boodle detested smoking, as a woman of her high principles should. She had an entire mastery over the worthy old gentleman, and thought I was a sort of demon of wickedness. The old man went to his grave with some similar notion,—heaven help him! and left me but the wretched twelve thousand pounds secured to me on my poor mother's property.

In the army, my luck was much the same. I joined the —th Lancers, Lieut.-Col. Lord Martingale, in the year 1817. I only did duty with the regiment for three months. We were quartered at Cork, where I found the Irish doodheen and tobacco the pleasantest smoking possible; and was found by his lordship, one day upon stable duty, smoking the shortest, dearest little dumpy clay-pipe in the world.

"Cornet Fitz-Boodle," said my lord in a towering passion, "from what blackguard did you get that pipe?"

I omit the oaths which garnished invariably his lordship's conversation.

"I got it, my lord," said I, "from one Terence Mullins, a jingle-driver, with a packet of his peculiar tobacco. You sometimes smoke Turkish, I believe; do try this. Isn't it good?" And in the simplest way in the world I puffed a volume into his face. "I see you like it," said I, so coolly, that the men—and I do believe the horses—burst out laughing.

He started back—choking almost, and recovered himself only to vent such a storm of oaths and curses that I was compelled to request Capt. Rawdon (the captain on duty) to take note of his lordship's words; and unluckily could not help adding a question which settled my business. "You were good enough," I said, "to ask me, my lord, from what blackguard I got my pipe; might I ask from what blackguard you learned your language?"

This was quite enough. Had I said, "from what GENTLEMAN did your lordship learn your language?" the point would have been quite as good, and my Lord Martingale would have suffered in my place: as it was, I was so strongly recommended to sell out by his Royal Highness the Commander-in-Chief, that, being of a good-natured disposition, never knowing how to refuse a friend, I at once threw up my hopes of military distinction and retired into civil life.

My lord was kind enough to meet me afterwards in a field in the Glanmire Road, where he put a ball into my leg. This I returned to him some years later with about twenty-three others—black ones—when he came to be balloted for at a club of which I have the honor to be a member.

Thus by the indulgence of a simple and harmless propensity,—of a propensity which can inflict an injury upon no person or thing except the coat and the person of him who indulges in it,—of a custom honored and observed in almost all the nations of the world,—of a custom which, far from leading a man into any wickedness or dissipation to which youth is subject, on the contrary, begets only benevolent silence, and thoughtful good-humored observation—I found at the age of twenty all my prospects in life destroyed. I cared not for woman in those days: the calm smoker has a sweet companion in his pipe. I did not drink immoderately of wine; for though a friend to trifling potations, to excessively strong drinks tobacco is abhorrent. I never thought of gambling, for the lover of the pipe has no need of such excitement; but I was considered a monster of dissipation in my family, and bade fair to come to ruin.

"Look at George," my mother-in-law said to the genteel and correct young Flintskinners. "He entered the world with every prospect in life, and see in what an abyss of degradation his fatal habits have plunged him! At school, he was flogged and disgraced, he was disgraced and rusticated at the university, he was disgraced and expelled from the army! He might have had the living of Boodle" (her ladyship gave it to one of her nephews), "but he would not take his degree; his papa would have purchased him a troop—nay, a lieutenant-colonelcy some day, but for his fatal excesses. And now as long as my dear husband will listen to the voice of a wife who adores him—never, never shall he spend a shilling upon so worthless a young man. He has a small income from his mother (I cannot but think that the first Lady Fitz-Boodle was a weak and misguided person); let him live upon his mean pittance as he can, and I heartily pray we may not hear of him in gaol!"

My brother, after he came to the estate, married the ninth daughter of our neighbor, Sir John Spreadeagle; and Boodle Hall has seen a new little Fitz-Boodle with every succeeding spring. The dowager retired to Scotland with a large jointure and a wondrous heap of savings. Lady Fitz is a good creature, but she thinks me something diabolical, trembles when she sees me, and gathers all her children about her, rushes into the nursery whenever I pay that little seminary a visit, and actually slapped poor little Frank's ears one day when I was teaching him to ride upon the back of a Newfoundland dog.

"George," said my brother to me the last time I paid him a visit at the old hall, "don't be angry, my dear fellow, but Maria is in a—hum—in a delicate situation, expecting her—hum"—(the eleventh)—"and do you know you frighten her? It was but yesterday you met her in the rookery—you were smoking that enormous German pipe—and when she came in she had an hysterical seizure, and Drench says that in her situation it's dangerous. And I say, George, if you go to town you'll find a couple of hundred at your banker's." And with this the poor fellow shook me by the hand, and called for a fresh bottle of claret.

Afterwards he told me, with many hesitations, that my room at Boodle Hall had been made into a second nursery. I see my sister-in-law in London twice or thrice in the season, and the little people, who have almost forgotten to call me uncle George.

It's hard, too, for I am a lonely man after all, and my heart yearns to them. The other day I smuggled a couple of them into my chambers, and had a little feast of cream and strawberries to welcome them. But it had like to have cost the nursery-maid (a Swiss girl that Fitz-Boodle hired somewhere in his travels) her place. My step-mamma, who happened to be in town, came flying down in her chariot, pounced upon the poor thing and the children in the midst of the entertainment; and when I asked her, with rather a bad grace to be sure, to take a chair and a share of the feast—"Mr. Fitz-Boodle," said she, "I am not accustomed to sit down in a place that smells of tobacco like an ale-house—an ale-house inhabited by a SERPENT, sir! A SERPENT!—do you understand me?—who carries his poison into his brother's own house, and purshues his eenfamous designs before his brother's own children. Put on Miss Maria's bonnet this instant. Mamsell, ontondy-voo? Metty le bonny a mamsell. And I shall take care, Mamsell, that you return to Switzerland to-morrow. I've no doubt you are a relation of Courvoisier—oui! oui! courvoisier, vous comprenny—and you shall certainly be sent back to your friends."

With this speech, and with the children and their maid sobbing before her, my lady retired; but for once my sister-in-law was on my side, not liking the meddlement of the elder lady.

I know, then, that from indulging in that simple habit of smoking, I have gained among the ladies a dreadful reputation. I see that they look coolly upon me, and darkly at their husbands when they arrive at home in my company. Men, I observe, in consequence, ask me to dine much oftener at the club, or the "Star and Garter" at Richmond, or at "Lovegrove's," than in their own houses; and with this sort of arrangement I am fain to acquiesce; for, as I said before, I am of an easy temper, and can at any rate take my cigar-case out after dinner at Blackwall, when my lady or the duchess is not by. I know, of course, the best MEN in town; and as for ladies' society, not having it (for I will have none of your pseudo-ladies, such as sometimes honor bachelors' parties,—actresses, couturieres, opera-dancers, and so forth)—as for ladies' society, I say, I cry pish! 'tis not worth the trouble of the complimenting, and the bother of pumps and black silk stockings.

Let any man remember what ladies' society was when he had an opportunity of seeing them among themselves, as What-d'ye-call'im does in the Thesmophoria—(I beg pardon, I was on the verge of a classical allusion, which I abominate)—I mean at that period of his life when the intellect is pretty acute, though the body is small—namely, when a young gentleman is about eleven years of age, dining at his father's table during the holidays, and is requested by his papa to quit the dinner-table when the ladies retire from it.

Corbleu! I recollect their whole talk as well as if it had been whispered but yesterday; and can see, after a long dinner, the yellow summer sun throwing long shadows over the lawn before the dining-room windows, and my poor mother and her company of ladies sailing away to the music-room in old Boodle Hall. The Countess Dawdley was the great lady in our county, a portly lady who used to love crimson satin in those days, and birds-of-paradise. She was flaxen-haired, and the Regent once said she resembled one of King Charles's beauties.

When Sir John Todcaster used to begin his famous story of the exciseman (I shall not tell it here, for very good reasons), my poor mother used to turn to Lady Dawdley, and give that mystic signal at which all females rise from their chairs. Tufthunt, the curate, would spring from his seat, and be sure to be the first to open the door for the retreating ladies; and my brother Tom and I, though remaining stoutly in our places, were speedily ejected from them by the governor's invariable remark, "Tom and George, if you have had QUITE enough of wine, you had better go and join your mamma." Yonder she marches, heaven bless her! through the old oak hall (how long the shadows of the antlers are on the wainscot, and the armor of Rollo Fitz-Boodle looks in the sunset as if it were emblazoned with rubies)—yonder she marches, stately and tall, in her invariable pearl-colored tabbinet, followed by Lady Dawdley, blazing like a flamingo; next comes Lady Emily Tufthunt (she was Lady Emily Flintskinner), who will not for all the world take precedence of rich, vulgar, kind, good-humored Mrs. COLONEL Grogwater, as she would be called, with a yellow little husband from Madras, who first taught me to drink sangaree. He was a new arrival in our county, but paid nobly to the hounds, and occupied hospitably a house which was always famous for its hospitality—Sievely Hall (poor Bob Cullender ran through seven thousand a year before he was thirty years old). Once when I was a lad, Colonel Grogwater gave me two gold mohurs out of his desk for whist-markers, and I'm sorry to say I ran up from Eton and sold them both for seventy-three shillings at a shop in Cornhill. But to return to the ladies, who are all this while kept waiting in the hall, and to their usual conversation after dinner.

Can any man forget how miserably flat it was? Five matrons sit on sofas, and talk in a subdued voice:—
First Lady (mysteriously).—"My dear Lady Dawdley, do tell me about poor Susan Tuckett."

Second Lady.—"All three children are perfectly well, and I assure you as fine babies as I ever saw in my life. I made her give them Daffy's Elixir the first day; and it was the greatest mercy that I had some of Frederick's baby-clothes by me; for you know I had provided Susan with sets for one only, and really—"

Third Lady.—"Of course one couldn't; and for my part I think your ladyship is a great deal too kind to these people. A little gardener's boy dressed in Lord Dawdley's frocks indeed! I recollect that one at his christening had the sweetest lace in the world!"

Fourth Lady.—"What do you think of this, ma'am—Lady Emily, I mean? I have just had it from Howell and James:—guipure, they call it. Isn't it an odd name for lace! And they charge me, upon my conscience, four guineas a yard!"

Third Lady.—"My mother, when she came to Flintskinner, had lace upon her robe that cost sixty guineas a yard, ma'am! 'Twas sent from Malines direct by our relation, the Count d'Araignay."

Fourth Lady (aside).—"I thought she would not let the evening pass without talking of her Malines lace and her Count d'Araignay. Odious people! they don't spare their backs, but they pinch their—"

Here Tom upsets a coffee-cup over his white jean trousers, and another young gentleman bursts into a laugh, saying, "By Jove, that's a good 'un!"

"George, my dear," says mamma, "had not you and your young friend better go into the garden? But mind, no fruit, or Dr. Glauber must be called in again immediately!" And we all go, and in ten minutes I and my brother are fighting in the stables.

If, instead of listening to the matrons and their discourse, we had taken the opportunity of attending to the conversation of the Misses, we should have heard matter not a whit more interesting.

First Miss.—"They were all three in blue crape; you never saw anything so odious. And I know for a certainty that they wore those dresses at Muddlebury, at the archery-ball, and I dare say they had them in town."

Second Miss.—"Don't you think Jemima decidedly crooked? And those fair complexions, they freckle so, that really Miss Blanche ought to be called Miss Brown."

Third Miss.—"He, he, he!"

Fourth Miss.—"Don't you think Blanche is a pretty name?"

First Miss.—"La! do you think so, dear? Why, it's my second name!"

Second Miss.—"Then I'm sure Captain Travers thinks it a BEAUTIFUL name!"

Third Miss.—"He, he, he!"

Fourth Miss.—"What was he telling you at dinner that seemed to interest you so?"

First Miss.—"O law, nothing!—that is, yes! Charles—that is,—Captain Travers, is a sweet poet, and was reciting to me some lines that he had composed upon a faded violet:—

"'The odor from the flower is gone,
That like thy—,

like thy something, I forget what it was; but his lines are sweet, and so original too! I wish that horrid Sir John Todcaster had not begun his story of the exciseman, for Lady Fitz-Boodle always quits the table when he begins."

Third Miss.—"Do you like those tufts that gentlemen wear sometimes on their chins?"

Second Miss.—"Nonsense, Mary!"

Third Miss.—"Well, I only asked, Jane. Frank thinks, you know, that he shall very soon have one, and puts bear's-grease on his chin every night."

Second Miss.—"Mary, nonsense!"

Third Miss.—"Well, only ask him. You know he came to our dressing-room last night and took the pomatum away; and he says that when boys go to Oxford they always—"

First Miss.—"O heavens! have you heard the news about the Lancers? Charles—that is, Captain Travers, told it me!"

Second Miss.—"Law! they won't go away before the ball, I hope!"

First Miss.—"No, but on the 15th they are to shave their moustaches! He says that Lord Tufto is in a perfect fury about it!"

Second Miss.—"And poor George Beardmore, too!" &c.

Here Tom upsets the coffee over his trousers, and the conversations end. I can recollect a dozen such, and ask any man of sense whether such talk amuses him?

Try again to speak to a young lady while you are dancing—what we call in this country—a quadrille. What nonsense do you invariably give and receive in return! No, I am a woman-scorner, and don't care to own it. I hate young ladies! Have I not been in love with several, and has any one of them ever treated me decently? I hate married women! Do they not hate me? and, simply because I smoke, try to draw their husbands away from my society? I hate dowagers! Have I not cause? Does not every dowager in London point to George Fitz-Boodle as to a dissolute wretch whom young and old should avoid?

And yet do not imagine that I have not loved. I have, and madly, many, many times! I am but eight-and-thirty,* not past the age of passion, and may very likely end by running off with an heiress—or a cook-maid (for who knows what strange freaks Love may choose to play in his own particular person? and I hold a man to be a mean creature who calculates about checking any such sacred impulse as lawful love)—I say, though despising the sex in general for their conduct to me, I know of particular persons belonging to it who are worthy of all respect and esteem, and as such I beg leave to point out the particular young lady who is perusing these lines. Do not, dear madam, then imagine that if I knew you I should be disposed to sneer at you. Ah, no! Fitz-Boodle's bosom has tenderer sentiments than from his way of life you would fancy, and stern by rule is only too soft by practice. Shall I whisper to you the story of one or two of my attachments? All terminating fatally (not in death, but in disappointment, which, as it occurred, I used to imagine a thousand times more bitter than death, but from which one recovers somehow more readily than from the other-named complaint)—all, I say, terminating wretchedly to myself, as if some fatality pursued my desire to become a domestic character.

* He is five-and-forty, if he is a day old.—O. Y.

My first love—no, let us pass THAT over. Sweet one! thy name shall profane no hireling page. Sweet, sweet memory! Ah, ladies, those delicate hearts of yours have, too, felt the throb. And between the last 'ob' in the word throb and the words now written, I have passed a delicious period of perhaps an hour, perhaps a minute, I know not how long, thinking of that holy first love and of her who inspired it. How clearly every single incident of the passion is remembered by me! and yet 'twas long, long since. I was but a child then—a child at school—and, if the truth must be told, L—ra R-ggl-s (I would not write her whole name to be made one of the Marquess of Hertford's executors) was a woman full thirteen years older than myself; at the period of which I write she must have been at least five-and-twenty. She and her mother used to sell tarts, hard-bake, lollipops, and other such simple comestibles, on Wednesdays and Saturdays (half-holidays), at a private school where I received the first rudiments of a classical education. I used to go and sit before her tray for hours, but I do not think the poor girl ever supposed any motive led me so constantly to her little stall beyond a vulgar longing for her tarts and her ginger-beer. Yes, even at that early period my actions were misrepresented, and the fatality which has oppressed my whole life began to show itself,—the purest passion was misinterpreted by her and my school-fellows, and they thought I was actuated by simple gluttony. They nicknamed me Alicompayne.

Well, be it so. Laugh at early passion ye who will; a highborn boy madly in love with a lowly ginger-beer girl! She married afterwards, took the name of Latter, and now keeps with her old husband a turnpike, through which I often ride; but I can recollect her bright and rosy of a sunny summer afternoon, her red cheeks shaded by a battered straw bonnet, her tarts and ginger-beer upon a neat white cloth before her, mending blue worsted stockings until the young gentlemen should interrupt her by coming to buy.

Many persons will call this description low; I do not envy them their gentility, and have always observed through life (as, to be sure, every other GENTLEMAN has observed as well as myself) that it is your parvenu who stickles most for what he calls the genteel, and has the most squeamish abhorrence for what is frank and natural. Let us pass at once, however, as all the world must be pleased, to a recital of an affair which occurred in the very best circles of society, as they are called, viz, my next unfortunate attachment.

It did not occur for several years after that simple and platonic passion just described: for though they may talk of youth as the season of romance, it has always appeared to me that there are no beings in the world so entirely unromantic and selfish as certain young English gentlemen from the age of fifteen to twenty. The oldest Lovelace about town is scarcely more hard-hearted and scornful than they; they ape all sorts of selfishness and rouerie: they aim at excelling at cricket, at billiards, at rowing, and drinking, and set more store by a red coat and a neat pair of top-boots than by any other glory. A young fellow staggers into college chapel of a morning, and communicates to all his friends that he was "so CUT last night," with the greatest possible pride. He makes a joke of having sisters and a kind mother at home who loves him; and if he speaks of his father, it is with a knowing sneer to say that he has a tailor's and a horse-dealer's bill that will surprise "the old governor." He would be ashamed of being in love. I, in common with my kind, had these affectations, and my perpetual custom of smoking added not a little to my reputation as an accomplished roue. What came of this custom in the army and at college, the reader has already heard. Alas! in life it went no better with me, and many pretty chances I had went off in that accursed smoke.

After quitting the army in the abrupt manner stated, I passed some short time at home, and was tolerated by my mother-in-law, because I had formed an attachment to a young lady of good connections and with a considerable fortune, which was really very nearly becoming mine. Mary M'Alister was the only daughter of Colonel M'Alister, late of the Blues, and Lady Susan his wife. Her ladyship was no more; and, indeed, of no family compared to ours (which has refused a peerage any time these two hundred years); but being an earl's daughter and a Scotchwoman, Lady Emily Fitz-Boodle did not fail to consider her highly. Lady Susan was daughter of the late Admiral Earl of Marlingspike and

Baron Plumduff. The Colonel, Miss M'Alister's father, had a good estate, of which his daughter was the heiress, and as I fished her out of the water upon a pleasure-party, and swam with her to shore, we became naturally intimate, and Colonel M'Alister forgot, on account of the service rendered to him, the dreadful reputation for profligacy which I enjoyed in the county.

Well, to cut a long story short, which is told here merely for the moral at the end of it, I should have been Fitz-Boodle M'Alister at this minute most probably, and master of four thousand a year, but for the fatal cigar-box. I bear Mary no malice in saying that she was a high-spirited little girl, loving, before all things, her own way; nay, perhaps I do not, from long habit and indulgence in tobacco-smoking, appreciate the delicacy of female organizations, which were oftentimes most painfully affected by it. She was a keen-sighted little person, and soon found that the world had belied poor George Fitz-Boodle; who, instead of being the cunning monster people supposed him to be, was a simple, reckless, good-humored, honest fellow, marvellously addicted to smoking, idleness, and telling the truth. She called me Orson, and I was happy enough on the 14th February, in the year 18— (it's of no consequence), to send her such a pretty little copy of verses about Orson and Valentine, in which the rude habits of the savage man were shown to be overcome by the polished graces of his kind and brilliant conqueror, that she was fairly overcome, and said to me, "George Fitz-Boodle, if you give up smoking for a year, I will marry you."

I swore I would, of course, and went home and flung four pounds of Hudson's cigars, two meerschaum pipes that had cost me ten guineas at the establishment of Mr. Gattie at Oxford, a tobacco-bag that Lady Fitz-Boodle had given me BEFORE her marriage with my father (it was the only present that I ever had from her or any member of the Flintskinner family), and some choice packets of Varinas and Syrian, into the lake in Boodle Park. The weapon amongst them all which I most regretted was—will it be believed?—the little black doodheen which had been the cause of the quarrel between Lord Martingale and me. However, it went along with the others. I would not allow my groom to have so much as a cigar, lest I should be tempted hereafter; and the consequence was that a few days after many fat carps and tenches in the lake (I must confess 'twas no bigger than a pond) nibbled at the tobacco, and came floating on their backs on the top of the water quite intoxicated. My conversion made some noise in the county, being emphasized as it were by this fact of the fish. I can't tell you with what pangs I kept my resolution; but keep it I did for some time.

With so much beauty and wealth, Mary M'Alister had of course many suitors, and among them was the young Lord Dawdley, whose mamma has previously been described in her gown of red satin. As I used to thrash Dawdley at school, I thrashed him in after-life in love; he put up with his disappointment pretty well, and came after a while and shook hands with me, telling me of the bets that there were in the county, where the whole story was known, for and against me. For the fact is, as I must own, that Mary M'Alister, the queerest, frankest of women, made no secret of the agreement, or the cause of it.

"I did not care a penny for Orson," she said, "but he would go on writing me such dear pretty verses that at last I couldn't help saying yes. But if he breaks his promise to me, I declare, upon my honor, I'll break mine, and nobody's heart will be broken either."

This was the perfect fact, as I must confess, and I declare that it was only because she amused me and delighted me, and provoked me, and made me laugh very much, and because, no doubt, she was very rich, that I had any attachment for her.

"For heaven's sake, George," my father said to me, as I quitted home to follow my beloved to London, "remember that you are a younger brother and have a lovely girl and four thousand a year within a year's reach of you. Smoke as much as you like, my boy, after marriage," added the old gentleman, knowingly (as if HE, honest soul, after his second marriage, dared drink an extra pint of wine without my lady's permission!) "but eschew the tobacco-shops till then."

I went to London resolving to act upon the paternal advice, and oh! how I longed for the day when I should be married, vowing in my secret soul that I would light a cigar as I walked out of St. George's, Hanover Square.

Well, I came to London, and so carefully avoided smoking that I would not even go into Hudson's shop to pay his bill, and as smoking was not the fashion then among young men as (thank heaven!) it is now, I had not many temptations from my friends' examples in my clubs or elsewhere; only little Dawdley began to smoke, as if to spite me. He had never done so before, but confessed—the rascal!—that he enjoyed a cigar now, if it were but to mortify me. But I took to other and more dangerous excitements, and upon the nights when not in attendance upon Mary M'Alister, might be found in very dangerous proximity to a polished mahogany table, round which claret-bottles circulated a great deal too often, or worse still, to a table covered with green cloth and ornamented with a couple of wax-candles and a couple of packs of cards, and four gentlemen playing the enticing game of whist. Likewise, I came to carry a snuff-box, and to consume in secret huge quantities of rappee.

For ladies' society I was even then disinclined, hating and despising small-talk, and dancing, and hot routs, and vulgar scrambles for suppers. I never could understand the pleasure of acting the part of lackey to a dowager, and standing behind her chair, or bustling through the crowd for her carriage. I always found an opera too long by two acts, and have repeatedly fallen asleep in the presence of Mary M'Alister herself, sitting at the back of the box shaded by the huge beret of her old aunt, Lady Betty Plumduff; and many a time has Dawdley, with Miss M'Alister on his arm, wakened me up at the close of the entertainment in time to offer my hand to Lady Betty, and lead the ladies to their carriage. If I attended her occasionally to any ball or party of pleasure, I went, it must be confessed, with clumsy, ill-disguised ill-humor. Good heavens! have I often and often thought in the midst of a song, or the very thick of a ball-room, can people prefer this to a book and a sofa, and a dear, dear cigar-box, from thy stores, O charming Mariana Woodville! Deprived of my favorite plant, I grew sick in mind and body, moody, sarcastic, and discontented.

Such a state of things could not long continue, nor could Miss M'Alister continue to have much attachment for such a sullen, ill-conditioned creature as I then was. She used to make me wild with her wit and her sarcasm, nor have I ever possessed the readiness to parry or reply to those fine points of woman's wit, and she treated me the more mercilessly as she saw that I could not resist her.

Well, the polite reader must remember a great fete that was given at B— House, some years back, in honor of his Highness the Hereditary Prince of Kalbsbraten-Pumpernickel, who was then in London on a visit to his illustrious relatives. It was a fancy ball, and the poems of Scott being at that time all the fashion, Mary was to appear in the character of the "Lady of the Lake," old M'Alister making a very tall and severe-looking harper; Dawdley, a most insignificant Fitzjames; and your humble servant a stalwart manly Roderick Dhu. We were to meet at B— House at twelve o'clock, and as I had no fancy to drive through the town in my cab dressed in a kilt and philibeg, I agreed to take a seat in Dawdley's carriage, and to dress at his house in May Fair. At eleven I left a very pleasant bachelors' party, growling to quit them and the honest, jovial claret-bottle, in order to scrape and cut capers like a harlequin from the theatre. When I arrived at Dawdley's, I mounted to a dressing-room, and began to array myself in my cursed costume.

The art of costuming was by no means so well understood in those days as it has been since, and mine was out of all correctness. I was made to sport an enormous plume of black ostrich-feathers, such as never was worn by any Highland chief, and had a huge tiger-skin sporran to dangle like an apron before innumerable yards of plaid petticoat. The tartan cloak was outrageously hot and voluminous; it was the dog-days, and all these things I was condemned to wear in the midst of a crowd of a thousand people!

Dawdley sent up word, as I was dressing, that his dress had not arrived, and he took my cab and drove off in a rage to his tailor.

There was no hurry, I thought, to make a fool of myself; so having put on a pair of plaid trews, and very neat pumps with shoe-buckles, my courage failed me as to the rest of the dress, and taking down one of his dressing-gowns, I went down stairs to the study, to wait until he should arrive.

The windows of the pretty room were open, and a snug sofa, with innumerable cushions, drawn towards one of them. A great tranquil moon was staring into the chamber, in which stood, amidst books and all sorts of bachelor's lumber, a silver tray with a couple of tall Venice glasses, and a bottle of Maraschino bound with straw. I can see now the twinkle of the liquor in the moonshine, as I poured it into the glass; and I swallowed two or three little cups of it, for my spirits were downcast. Close to the tray of Maraschino stood—must I say it?—a box, a mere box of cedar, bound rudely together with pink paper, branded with the name of "Hudson" on the side, and bearing on the cover the arms of Spain. I thought I would just take up the box and look in it.

Ah heaven! there they were—a hundred and fifty of them, in calm, comfortable rows: lovingly side by side they lay, with the great moon shining down upon them—thin at the tip, full in the waist, elegantly round and full, a little spot here and there shining upon them—beauty-spots upon the cheek of Sylvia. The house was quite quiet. Dawdley always smoked in his room—I had not smoked for four months and eleven days.

When Lord Dawdley came into the study, he did not make any remarks; and oh, how easy my heart felt! He was dressed in his green and boots, after Westall's picture, correctly.

"It's time to be off, George," said he; "they told me you were dressed long ago. Come up, my man, and get ready."

I rushed up into the dressing-room, and madly dashed my head and arms into a pool of eau-de-Cologne. I drank, I believe, a tumberful of it. I called for my clothes, and, strange to say, they were gone. My servant brought them, however, saying that he had put them away—making some stupid excuse. I put them on, not heeding them much, for I was half tipsy with the excitement of the ci— of the smo— of what had taken place in Dawdley's study, and with the Maraschino and the eau-de-Cologue I had drunk.

"What a fine odor of lavender-water!" said Dawdley, as we rode in the carriage.

I put my head out of the window and shrieked out a laugh; but made no other reply.

"What's the joke, George?" said Dawdley. "Did I say anything witty?"

"No," cried I, yelling still more wildly; "nothing more witty than usual."

"Don't be severe, George," said he, with a mortified air; and we drove on to B— House.

There must have been something strange and wild in my appearance, and those awful black plumes, as I passed through the crowd; for I observed people looking and making a strange nasal noise (it is called sniffing, and I have no other more delicate term for it), and making way as I pushed on. But I moved forward very fiercely, for the wine, the Maraschino, the eau-de-Cologne, and the—the excitement had rendered me almost wild; and at length I arrived at the place where my lovely Lady of the Lake and her Harper stood. How beautiful she looked,—all eyes were upon her as she stood blushing. When she saw me, however; her countenance assumed an appearance of alarm. "Good heavens, George!" she said, stretching her hand to me, "what makes you look so wild and pale?" I advanced, and was going to take her hand, when she dropped it with a scream.

"Ah—ah—ah!" she said. "Mr. Fitz-Boodle, you've been smoking!"

There was an immense laugh from four hundred people round about us, and the scoundrelly Dawdley joined in the yell. I rushed furiously out, and, as I passed, hurtled over the fat Hereditary Prince of Kalbsbraten-Pumpernickel.

"Es riecht hier ungeheuer stark von Tabak!" I heard his Highness say, as I madly flung myself through the aides-de-camp.

The next day Mary M'Alister, in a note full of the most odious good sense and sarcasm, reminded me of our agreement; said that she was quite convinced that we were not by any means fitted for one another, and begged me to consider myself henceforth quite free. The little wretch had the impertinence to send me a dozen boxes of cigars, which, she said, would console me for my lost love; as she was perfectly certain that I was not mercenary, and that I loved tobacco better than any woman in the world.

I believe she was right, though I have never to this day been able to pardon the scoundrelly stratagem by which Dawdley robbed me of a wife and won one himself. As I was lying on his sofa, looking at the moon and lost in a thousand happy contemplations, Lord Dawdley, returning from the tailor's, saw me smoking at my leisure. On entering his dressing-room, a horrible treacherous thought struck him. "I must not betray my friend," said he; "but in love all is fair, and he shall betray himself." There were my tartans, my cursed feathers, my tiger-skin sporran, upon the sofa.

He called up my groom; he made the rascal put on all my clothes, and, giving him a guinea and four cigars, bade him lock himself into the little pantry and smoke them WITHOUT TAKING THE CLOTHES OFF. John did so, and was very ill in consequence, and so when I came to B— House, my clothes were redolent of tobacco, and I lost lovely Mary M'Alister.

I am godfather to one of Lady Dawdley's boys, and hers is the only house where I am allowed to smoke unmolested; but I have never been able to admire Dawdley, a sly, sournois, spiritless, lily-livered fellow, that took his name off all his clubs the year he married.

DOROTHEA

Beyond sparring and cricket, I do not recollect I learned anything useful at Slaughter-House School, where I was educated (according to an old family tradition, which sends particular generations of gentlemen to particular schools in the kingdom; and such is the force of habit, that though I hate the place, I shall send my own son thither too, should I marry any day). I say I learned little that was useful at Slaughter House, and nothing that was ornamental. I would as soon have thought of learning to dance as of learning to climb chimneys. Up to the age of seventeen, as I have shown, I had a great contempt for the female race, and when age brought with it warmer and juster sentiments, where was I?—I could no more dance nor prattle to a young girl than a young bear could. I have seen the ugliest little low-bred wretches carrying off young and lovely creatures, twirling with them in waltzes, whispering between their glossy curls in quadrilles, simpering with perfect equanimity, and cutting pas in that abominable "cavalier seul," until my soul grew sick with fury. In a word, I determined to learn to dance.

But such things are hard to be acquired late in life, when the bones and the habits of a man are formed. Look at a man in a hunting-field who has not been taught to ride as a boy. All the pluck and courage in the world will not make the man of him that I am, or as any man who has had the advantages of early education in the field.

In the same way with dancing. Though I went to work with immense energy, both in Brewer Street, Golden Square (with an advertising fellow), and afterwards with old Coulon at Paris, I never was able to be EASY in dancing; and though little Coulon instructed me in a smile, it was a cursed forced one, that looked like the grin of a person in extreme agony. I once caught sight of it in a glass, and have hardly ever smiled since.

Most young men about London have gone through that strange secret ordeal of the dancing-school. I am given to understand that young snobs from attorneys' offices, banks, shops, and the like, make not the least mystery of their proceedings in the saltatory line, but trip gayly, with pumps in hand, to some dancing-place about Soho, waltz and quadrille it with Miss Greengrocer or Miss Butcher, and fancy they have had rather a pleasant evening. There is one house in Dover Street, where, behind a dirty curtain, such figures may be seen hopping every night, to a perpetual fiddling; and I have stood sometimes wondering in the street, with about six blackguard boys wondering too, at the strange contortions of the figures jumping up and down to the mysterious squeaking of the kit. Have they no shame ces gens? are such degrading initiations to be held in public? No, the snob may, but the man of refined mind never can submit to show himself in public laboring at the apprenticeship of this most absurd art. It is owing, perhaps, to this modesty, and the fact that I had no sisters at home, that I have never thoroughly been able to dance; for though I always arrive at the end of a quadrille (and thank heaven for it too!) and though, I believe, I make no mistake in particular, yet I solemnly confess I have never been able thoroughly to comprehend the mysteries of it, or what I have been about from the beginning to the end of the dance. I always look at the lady opposite, and do as she does: if SHE did not know how to dance, par hasard, it would be all up. But if they can't do anything else, women can dance: let us give them that praise at least.

In London, then, for a considerable time, I used to get up at eight o'clock in the morning, and pass an hour alone with Mr. Wilkinson, of the Theatres Royal, in Golden Square;—an hour alone. It was "one, two, three; one, two, three—now jump—right foot more out, Mr. Smith; and if you COULD try and look a little more cheerful; your partner, sir, would like you hall the better." Wilkinson called me Smith, for the fact is, I did not tell him my real name, nor (thank heaven!) does he know it to this day.

I never breathed a word of my doings to any soul among my friends; once a pack of them met me in the strange neighborhood, when, I am ashamed to say, I muttered something about a "little French milliner," and walked off, looking as knowing as I could.

In Paris, two Cambridge-men and myself, who happened to be staying at a boarding-house together, agreed to go to Coulon, a little creature of four feet high with a pigtail. His room was hung round with glasses. He made us take off our coats, and dance each before a mirror. Once he was standing before us playing on his kit the sight of the little master and the pupil was so supremely ridiculous, that I burst into a yell of laughter, which so offended the old man that he walked away abruptly, and begged me not to repeat my visits. Nor did I. I was just getting into waltzing then, but determined to drop waltzing, and content myself with quadrilling for the rest of my days.

This was all very well in France and England; but in Germany what was I to do? What did Hercules do when Omphale captivated him? What did Rinaldo do when Armida fixed upon him her twinkling eyes? Nay, to cut all historical instances short, by going at once to the earliest, what did Adam do when Eve tempted him? He yielded and became her slave; and so I do heartily trust every honest man will yield until the end of the world—he has no heart who will not. When I was in Germany, I say, I began to learn to WALTZ. The reader from this will no doubt expect that some new love-adventures befell me—nor will his gentle heart be disappointed. Two deep and tremendous incidents occurred which shall be notified on the present occasion.

The reader, perhaps, remembers the brief appearance of his Highness the Duke of Kalbsbraten-Pumpernickel at B— House, in the first part of my Memoirs, at that unlucky period of my life when the Duke was led to remark the odor about my clothes, which lost me the hand of Mary M'Alister. I somehow found myself in his Highness's territories, of which anybody may read a description in the Almanach de Gotha. His Highness's father, as is well known, married Emilia Kunegunda Thomasina Charleria Emanuela Louisa Georgina, Princess of Saxe-Pumpernickel, and a cousin of his Highness the Duke. Thus the two principalities were united under one happy sovereign in the person of Philibert Sigismund Emanuel Maria, the reigning Duke, who has received from his country (on account of the celebrated pump which he erected in the marketplace of Kalbsbraten) the well-merited appellation of the Magnificent. The allegory which the statues round about the pump represent, is of a very mysterious and complicated sort. Minerva is observed leading up Ceres to a river-god, who has his arms round the neck of Pomona; while Mars (in a full-bottomed wig) is driven away by Peace, under whose mantle two lovely children, representing the Duke's two provinces, repose. The celebrated Speck is, as need scarcely be said, the author of this piece; and of other magnificent edifices in the Residenz, such as the guard-room, the skittle-hall Grossherzoglich Kalbsbratenpumpernickelisch Schkittelspielsaal, &c., and the superb sentry-boxes before the Grand-Ducal Palace. He is Knight Grand Cross of the Ancient Kartoffel Order, as, indeed, is almost every one else in his Highness's dominions.

The town of Kalbsbraten contains a population of two thousand inhabitants, and a palace which would accommodate about six times that number. The principality sends three and a half men to the German Confederation, who are commanded by a General (Excellency), two Major-Generals, and sixty-four officers of lower grades; all noble, all knights of the Order, and almost all chamberlains to his Highness the Grand Duke. An excellent band of eighty performers is the admiration of the surrounding country, and leads the Grand-Ducal troops to battle in time of war. Only three of the contingent of soldiers returned from the Battle of Waterloo, where they won much honor; the remainder was cut to pieces on that glorious day.

There is a chamber of representatives (which, however, nothing can induce to sit), home and foreign ministers, residents from neighboring courts, law presidents, town councils, &c., all the adjuncts of a big or little government. The court has its chamberlains and marshals, the Grand Duchess her noble ladies in waiting, and blushing maids of honor. Thou wert one, Dorothea! Dost remember the poor young Englander? We parted in anger; but I think—I think thou hast not forgotten him.

The way in which I have Dorothea von Speck present to my mind is this: not as I first saw her in the garden—for her hair was in bandeaux then, and a large Leghorn hat with a deep ribbon covered half her fair face,—not in a morning-dress, which, by the way, was none of the newest nor the best made—but as I saw her afterwards at a ball at the pleasant splendid little court, where she moved the most beautiful of the beauties of Kalbsbraten. The grand saloon of the palace is lighted—the Grand Duke and his officers, the Duchess and her ladies, have passed through. I, in my uniform, of the —th, and a number of young fellows (who are evidently admiring my legs and envying my distingue appearance), are waiting round the entrance-door, where a huge Heyduke is standing, and announcing the titles of the guests as they arrive.

"HERR OBERHOF-UND BAU-INSPEKTOR VON SPECK!" shouts the Heyduke; and the little Inspector comes in. His lady is on his arm huge, in towering plumes, and her favorite costume of light blue. Fair women always dress in light blue or light green; and Frau von Speck is very fair and stout.

But who comes behind her? Lieber Himmel! It is Dorothea! Did earth, among all the flowers which have sprung from its bosom, produce ever one more beautiful? She was none of your heavenly beauties, I tell you. She had nothing ethereal about her. No, sir; she was of the earth earthy, and must have weighed ten stone four or five, if she weighed an ounce. She had none of your Chinese feet, nor waspy, unhealthy waists, which those may admire who will. No: Dora's foot was a good stout one; you could see her ankle (if her robe was short enough) without the aid of a microscope; and that envious little, sour, skinny Amalia von Mangelwurzel used to hold up her four fingers and say (the two girls were most intimate friends of course), "Dear Dorothea's vaist is so much dicker as dis." And so I have no doubt it was.

But what then? Goethe sings in one of his divine epigrams:—

"Epicures vaunting their taste, entitle me vulgar and savage, Give them their Brussels-sprouts, but I am contented with cabbage."

I hate your little women—that is, when I am in love with a tall one; and who would not have loved Dorothea?

Fancy her, then, if you please, about five feet four inches high—fancy her in the family color of light blue, a little scarf covering the most brilliant shoulders in the world; and a pair of gloves clinging close round an arm that may, perhaps, be somewhat too large now, but that Juno might have envied then. After the fashion of young ladies on the continent, she wears no jewels or gimcracks: her only ornament is a wreath of vine-leaves in her hair, with little clusters of artificial grapes. Down on her shoulders falls the brown hair, in rich liberal clusters; all that health, and good-humor, and beauty can do for her face, kind nature has done for hers. Her eyes are frank, sparkling, and kind. As for her cheeks, what paint-box or dictionary contains pigments or words to describe their red? They say she opens her mouth and smiles always to show the dimples in her cheeks. Psha! she smiles because she is happy, and kind, and good-humored, and not because her teeth are little pearls.

All the young fellows crowd up to ask her to dance, and, taking from her waist a little mother-of-pearl remembrancer, she notes them down. Old Schnabel for the polonaise; Klingenspohr, first waltz; Haarbart, second waltz; Count Hornpieper (the Danish envoy), third; and so on. I have said why I could not ask her to waltz, and I turned away with a pang, and played ecarte with Colonel Trumpenpack all night.

In thus introducing this lovely creature in her ball-costume, I have been somewhat premature, and had best go back to the beginning of the history of my acquaintance with her.

Dorothea, then, was the daughter of the celebrated Speck before mentioned. It is one of the oldest names in Germany, where her father's and mother's houses, those of Speck and Eyer, are loved wherever they are known. Unlike his warlike progenitor, Lorenzo von Speck, Dorothea's father, had early shown himself a passionate admirer of art; had quitted home to study architecture in Italy, and had become celebrated throughout Europe, and been appointed Oberhofarchitect and Kunst- und Bau-inspektor of the united principalities. They are but four miles wide, and his genius has consequently but little room to play. What art can do, however, he does. The palace is frequently whitewashed under his eyes; the theatre painted occasionally; the noble public buildings erected, of which I have already made mention.

I had come to Kalbsbraten, scarce knowing whither I went; and having, in about ten minutes, seen the curiosities of the place (I did not care to see the King's palace, for chairs and tables have no great charm for me), I had ordered horses, and wanted to get on I cared not whither, when Fate threw Dorothea in my way. I was yawning back to the hotel through the palace-garden, a valet-de-place at my side, when I saw a young lady seated under a tree reading a novel, her mamma on the same bench (a fat woman in light blue) knitting a stocking, and two officers, choked in their stays, with various orders on their spinach-colored coats, standing by in first attitudes: the one was caressing the fat-lady-in-blue's little dog; the other was twirling his own moustache, which was already as nearly as possible curled into his own eye.

I don't know how it is, but I hate to see men evidently intimate with nice-looking women, and on good terms with themselves. There's something annoying in their cursed complacency—their evident sunshiny happiness. I've no woman to make sunshine for ME; and yet my heart tells me that not one, but several such suns, would do good to my system.

"Who are those pert-looking officers," says I, peevishly, to the guide, "who are talking to those vulgar-looking women?"

"The big one, with the epaulets, is Major von Schnabel; the little one, with the pale face, is Stiefel von Klingenspohr."

"And the big blue woman?"

"The Grand-Ducal Pumpernickelian-court-architectress and Upper-Palace-and-building-inspectress Von Speck, born V. Eyer," replied the guide. "Your well-born honor has seen the pump in the market-place; that is the work of the great Von Speck."

"And yonder young person?"

"Mr. Court-architect's daughter; the Fraulein Dorothea."

Dorothea looked up from her novel here, and turned her face towards the stranger who was passing, and then blushing turned it down again. Schnabel looked at me with a scowl, Klingenspohr with a simper, the dog with a yelp, the fat lady in blue just gave one glance, and seemed, I thought, rather well pleased. "Silence, Lischen!" said she to the dog. "Go on, darling Dorothea," she added, to her daughter, who continued her novel.

Her voice was a little tremulous, but very low and rich. For some reason or other, on getting back to the inn, I countermanded the horses, and said I would stay for the night.

I not only stayed that night, but many, many afterwards; and as for the manner in which I became acquainted with the Speck family, why it was a good joke against me at the time, and I did not like then to have it known; but now it may as well come out at once. Speck, as everybody knows, lives in the market-place, opposite his grand work of art, the town pump, or fountain. I bought a large sheet of paper, and having a knack at drawing, sat down, with the greatest gravity, before the pump, and sketched it for several hours. I knew it would bring out old Speck to see. At first he contented himself by flattening his nose against the window-glasses of his study, and looking what the Englander was about. Then he put on his gray cap with the huge green shade, and sauntered to the door: then he walked round me, and formed one of a band of street-idlers who were looking on: then at last he could restrain himself no more, but, pulling off his cap, with a low bow, began to discourse upon arts, and architecture in particular.

"It is curious," says he, "that you have taken the same view of which a print has been engraved."

"That IS extraordinary," says I (though it wasn't, for I had traced my drawing at a window off the very print in question). I added that I was, like all the world, immensely struck with the beauty of the edifice; heard of it at Rome, where it was considered to be superior to any of the celebrated fountains of that capital of the fine arts; finally, that unless perhaps the celebrated fountain of Aldgate in London might compare with it, Kalbsbraten building, EXCEPT in that case, was incomparable.

This speech I addressed in French, of which the worthy Hofarchitect understood somewhat, and continuing to reply in German, our conversation grew pretty close. It is singular that I can talk to a man and pay him compliments with the utmost gravity, whereas, to a woman, I at once lose all self-possession, and have never said a pretty thing in my life.

My operations on old Speck were so conducted, that in a quarter of an hour I had elicited from him an invitation to go over the town with him, and see its architectural beauties. So we walked through the huge half-furnished chambers of the palace, we panted up the copper pinnacle of the church-tower, we went to see the Museum and Gymnasium, and coming back into the market-place again, what could the Hofarchitect do but offer me a glass of wine and a seat in his house? He introduced me to his Gattinn, his Leocadia (the fat woman in blue), "as a young world-observer, and worthy art-friend, a young scion of British Adel, who had come to refresh himself at the Urquellen of his race, and see his brethren of the great family of Hermann."

I saw instantly that the old fellow was of a romantic turn, from this rodomontade to his lady; nor was she a whit less so; nor was Dorothea less sentimental than her mamma. She knew everything regarding the literature of Albion, as she was pleased to call it; and asked me news of all the famous writers there. I told her that Miss Edgeworth was one of the loveliest young beauties at our court; I described to her Lady Morgan, herself as beautiful as the wild Irish girl she drew; I promised to give her a signature of Mrs. Hemans (which I wrote for her that very evening); and described a fox-hunt, at which I had seen Thomas Moore and Samuel Rogers, Esquires; and a boxing-match, in which the athletic author of "Pelham" was pitched against the hardy mountain bard, Wordsworth. You see my education was not neglected, for though I have never read the works of the above-named ladies and gentlemen, yet I knew their names well enough.

Time passed away. I, perhaps, was never so brilliant in conversation as when excited by the Asmanshauser and the brilliant eyes of Dorothea that day. She and her parents had dined at their usual heathen hour; but I was, I don't care to own it, so smitten, that for the first time in my life I did not even miss the meal, and talked on until six o'clock, when tea was served. Madame Speck said they always drank it; and so placing a teaspoonful of bohea in a cauldron of water, she placidly handed out this decoction, which we took with cakes and tartines. I leave you to imagine how disgusted Klingenspohr and Schnabel looked when they stepped in as usual that evening to make their party of whist with the Speck family! Down they were obliged to sit; and the lovely Dorothea, for that night, declined to play altogether, and—sat on the sofa by me.

What we talked about, who shall tell? I would not, for my part, break the secret of one of those delicious conversations, of which I and every man in his time have held so many. You begin, very probably, about the weather—'tis a common subject, but what sentiments the genius of Love can fling into it! I have often, for my part, said to the girl of my heart for the time being, "It's a fine day," or "It's a rainy morning!" in a way that has brought tears to her eyes. Something beats in your heart, and twangle! a corresponding string thrills and echoes in hers. You offer her anything—her knitting-needles, a slice of bread-and-butter—what causes the grateful blush with which she accepts the one or the other? Why, she sees your heart handed over to her upon the needles, and the bread-and-butter is to her a sandwich with love inside it. If you say to your grandmother, "Ma'am, it's a fine day," or what not, she would find in the words no other meaning than their outward and visible one; but say so to the girl you love, and she understands a thousand mystic meanings in them. Thus, in a word, though Dorothea and I did not, probably, on the first night of our meeting, talk of anything more than the weather, or trumps, or some subjects which to such listeners as Schnabel and Klingenspohr and others might appear quite ordinary, yet to US they had a different signification, of which Love alone held the key.

Without further ado then, after the occurrences of that evening, I determined on staying at Kalbsbraten, and presenting my card the next day to the Hof-Marshal, requesting to have the honor of being presented to his Highness the Prince, at one of whose court-balls my Dorothea appeared as I have described her.

It was summer when I first arrived at Kalbsbraten. The little court was removed to Siegmundslust, his Highness's country-seat: no balls were taking place, and, in consequence, I held my own with Dorothea pretty well. I treated her admirer, Lieutenant Klingenspohr, with perfect scorn, had a manifest advantage over Major Schnabel, and used somehow to meet the fair one every day, walking in company with her mamma in the palace garden, or sitting under the acacias, with Belotte in her mother's lap, and the favorite romance beside her. Dear, dear Dorothea! what a number of novels she must have read in her time! She confesses to me that she had been in love with Uncas, with Saint Preux, with Ivanhoe, and with hosts of German heroes of romance; and when I asked her if she, whose heart was so tender towards imaginary youths, had never had a preference for any one of her living adorers, she only looked, and blushed, and sighed, and said nothing.

You see I had got on as well as man could do, until the confounded court season and the balls began, and then—why, then came my usual luck.

Waltzing is a part of a German girl's life. With the best will in the world—which, I doubt not, she entertains for me, for I never put the matter of marriage directly to her—Dorothea could not go to balls and not waltz. It was madness to me to see her whirling round the room with officers, attaches, prim little chamberlains with gold keys and embroidered coats, her hair floating in the wind, her hand reposing upon the abominable little dancer's epaulet, her good-humored face lighted up with still greater satisfaction. I saw that I must learn to waltz too, and took my measures accordingly.

The leader of the ballet at the Kalbsbraten theatre in my time was Springbock, from Vienna. He had been a regular zephyr once, 'twas said, in his younger days; and though he is now fifteen stone weight, I can, helas! recommend him conscientiously as a master; and I determined to take some lessons from him in the art which I had neglected so foolishly in early life.

It may be said, without vanity, that I was an apt pupil, and in the course of half a dozen lessons I had arrived at very considerable agility in the waltzing line, and could twirl round the room with him at such a pace as made the old gentleman pant again, and hardly left him breath enough to puff out a compliment to his pupil. I may say, that in a single week I became an expert waltzer; but as I wished, when I came out publicly in that character, to be quite sure of myself, and as I had hitherto practised not with a lady, but with a very fat old man, it was agreed that he should bring a lady of his acquaintance to perfect me, and accordingly, at my eighth lesson, Madame Springbock herself came to the dancing-room, and the old zephyr performed on the violin.

If any man ventures the least sneer with regard to this lady, or dares to insinuate anything disrespectful to her or myself, I say at once that he is an impudent calumniator. Madame Springbock is old enough to be my grandmother, and as ugly a woman as I ever saw; but, though old, she was passionnee pour la danse, and not having (on account, doubtless, of her age and unprepossessing appearance) many opportunities of indulging in her favorite pastime, made up for lost time by immense activity whenever she could get a partner. In vain, at the end of the hour, would Springbock exclaim, "Amalia, my soul's blessing, the time is up!" "Play on, dear Alphonso!" would the old lady exclaim, whisking me round: and though I had not the least pleasure in such a homely partner, yet for the sake of perfecting myself I waltzed and waltzed with her, until we were both half dead with fatigue.

At the end of three weeks I could waltz as well as any man in Germany.

At the end of four weeks there was a grand ball at court in honor of H. H. the Prince of Dummerland and his Princess, and THEN I determined I would come out in public. I dressed myself with unusual care and splendor. My hair was curled and my moustache dyed to a nicety; and of the four hundred gentlemen present, if the girls of Kalbsbraten DID select one who wore an English hussar uniform, why should I disguise the fact? In spite of my silence, the news had somehow got abroad, as news will in such small towns,—Herr von Fitz-Boodle was coming out in a waltz that evening. His Highness the Duke even made an allusion to the circumstance. When on this eventful night, I went, as usual, and made him my bow in the presentation, "Vous, monsieur," said he—"vous qui etes si jeune, devez aimer la danse." I blushed as red as my trousers, and bowing, went away.

I stepped up to Dorothea. Heavens! how beautiful she looked! and how archly she smiled as, with a thumping heart, I asked her hand for a WALTZ! She took out her little mother-of-pearl dancing-book, she wrote down my name with her pencil: we were engaged for the fourth waltz, and till then I left her to other partners.

Who says that his first waltz is not a nervous moment? I vow I was more excited than by any duel I ever fought. I would not dance any contre-danse or galop. I repeatedly went to the buffet and got glasses of punch (dear simple Germany! 'tis with rum-punch and egg-flip thy children strengthen themselves for the dance!) I went into the ball-room and looked—the couples bounded before me, the music clashed and rung in my ears—all was fiery, feverish, indistinct. The gleaming white columns, the polished oaken floors in which the innumerable tapers were reflected—all together swam before my eyes, and I was in a pitch of madness almost when the fourth waltz at length came. "WILL YOU DANCE WITH YOUR SWORD ON?" said the sweetest voice in the world. I blushed, and stammered, and trembled, as I laid down that weapon and my cap, and hark! the music began!

Oh, how my hand trembled as I placed it round the waist of Dorothea! With my left hand I took her right—did she squeeze it? I think she did—to this day I think she did. Away we went! we tripped over the polished oak floor like two young fairies. "Courage, monsieur," said she, with her sweet smile. Then it was "Tres bien, monsieur." Then I heard the voices humming and buzzing about. "Il danse bien, l'Anglais." "Ma foi, oui," says another. On we went, twirling and twisting, and turning and whirling; couple after couple dropped panting off. Little Klingenspohr himself was obliged to give in. All eyes were upon us—we were going round ALONE. Dorothea was almost exhausted, when

I have been sitting for two hours since I marked the asterisks, thinking—thinking. I have committed crimes in my life—who hasn't? But talk of remorse, what remorse is there like THAT which rushes up in a flood to my brain sometimes when I am alone, and causes me to blush when I'm a-bed in the dark?

I fell, sir, on that infernal slippery floor. Down we came like shot; we rolled over and over in the midst of the ballroom, the music going ten miles an hour, 800 pairs of eyes fixed upon us, a cursed shriek of laughter bursting out from all sides. Heavens! how clear I heard it, as we went on rolling and rolling! "My child! my Dorothea!" shrieked out Madame Speck, rushing forward, and as soon as she had breath to do so, Dorothea of course screamed too; then she fainted, then she was disentangled from out my spurs, and borne off by a bevy of tittering women. "Clumsy brute!" said Madame Speck, turning her fat back upon me. I remained upon my seant, wild, ghastly, looking about. It was all up with me—I knew it was. I wished I could have died there, and I wish so still.

Klingenspohr married her, that is the long and short; but before that event I placed a sabre-cut across the young scoundrel's nose, which destroyed HIS beauty for ever.

O Dorothea! you can't forgive me—you oughtn't to forgive me; but I love you madly still.

My next flame was Ottilia: but let us keep her for another number; my feelings overpower me at present.

CHAPTER I

THE ALBUM—THE MEDITERRANEAN HEATH

Travelling some little time back in a wild part of Connemara, where I had been for fishing and seal-shooting, I had the good luck to get admission to the chateau of a hospitable Irish gentleman, and to procure some news of my once dear Ottilia.

Yes, of no other than Ottilia v. Schlippenschlopp, the Muse of Kalbsbraten-Pumpernickel, the friendly little town far away in Sachsenland,—where old Speck built the town pump, where Klingenspohr was slashed across the nose,—where Dorothea rolled over and over in that horrible waltz with Fitz-Boo—Psha!—away with the recollection; but wasn't it strange to get news of Ottilia in the wildest corner of Ireland, where I never should have thought to hear her gentle name? Walking on that very Urrisbeg Mountain under whose shadow I heard Ottilia's name, Mackay, the learned author of the "Flora Patlandica," discovered the Mediterranean heath,—such a flower as I have often plucked on the sides of Vesuvius, and as Proserpine, no doubt, amused herself in gathering as she strayed in the fields of Enna. Here it is—the self-same flower, peering out at the Atlantic from Roundstone Bay; here, too, in this wild lonely place, nestles the fragrant memory of my Ottilia!

In a word, after a day on Ballylynch Lake (where, with a brown fly and a single hair, I killed fourteen salmon, the smallest twenty-nine pounds weight, the largest somewhere about five stone ten), my young friend Blake Bodkin Lynch Browne (a fine lad who has made his continental tour) and I adjourned, after dinner, to the young gentleman's private room, for the purpose of smoking a certain cigar; which is never more pleasant than after a hard day's sport, or a day spent in-doors, or after a good dinner, or a bad one, or at night when you are tired, or in the morning when you are fresh, or of a cold winter's day, or of a scorching summer's afternoon, or at any other moment you choose to fix upon.

What should I see in Blake's room but a rack of pipes, such as are to be found in almost all the bachelors' rooms in Germany, and amongst them was a porcelain pipe-head bearing the image of the Kalbsbraten pump! There it was: the old spout, the old familiar allegory of Mars, Bacchus, Apollo virorum, and the rest, that I had so often looked at from Hofarchitect Speck's window, as I sat there, by the side of Dorothea. The old gentleman had given me one of these very pipes; for he had hundreds of them painted, wherewith he used to gratify almost every stranger who came into his native town.

Any old place with which I have once been familiar (as, perhaps, I have before stated in these "Confessions"—but never mind that) is in some sort dear to me: and were I Lord Shootingcastle or Colonel Popland, I think after a residence of six months there I should love the Fleet Prison. As I saw the old familiar pipe, I took it down, and crammed it with Cavendish tobacco, and lay down on a sofa, and puffed away for an hour wellnigh, thinking of old, old times.

"You're very entertaining to-night, Fitz," says young Blake, who had made several tumblers of punch for me, which I had gulped down without saying a word. "Don't ye think ye'd be more easy in bed than snorting and sighing there on my sofa, and groaning fit to make me go hang myself?"

"I am thinking, Blake," says I, "about Pumpernickel, where old Speck gave you this pipe."

"'Deed he did," replies the young man; "and did ye know the old Bar'n?"

"I did," said I. "My friend, I have been by the banks of the Bendemeer. Tell me, are the nightingales still singing there, and do the roses still bloom?"

"The HWHAT?" cries Blake. "What the divvle, Fitz, are you growling about? Bendemeer Lake's in Westmoreland, as I preshume; and as for roses and nightingales, I give ye my word it's Greek ye're talking to me." And Greek it very possibly was, for my young friend, though as good across country as any man in his county, has not the fine feeling and tender perception of beauty which may be found elsewhere, dear madam.

"Tell me about Speck, Blake, and Kalbsbraten, and Dorothea, and Klingenspohr her husband."

"He with the cut across the nose, is it?" cries Blake. "I know him well, and his old wife."

"His old what, sir!" cries Fitz-Boodle, jumping up from his seat. "Klingenspohr's wife old!—is he married again?—Is Dorothea, then, d-d-dead?"

"Dead!—no more dead than you are, only I take her to be five-and-thirty. And when a woman has had nine children, you know, she looks none the younger; and I can tell ye that when she trod on my corruns at a ball at the Grand Juke's, I felt something heavier than a feather on my foot."

"Madame de Klingenspohr, then," replied I, hesitating somewhat, "has grown rather—rather st-st-out?" I could hardly get out the OUT, and trembled I don't know why as I asked the question.

"Stout, begad!—she weighs fourteen stone, saddle and bridle. That's right, down goes my pipe; flop! crash falls the tumbler into the fender! Break away, my boy, and remember, whoever breaks a glass here pays a dozen."

The fact was, that the announcement of Dorothea's changed condition caused no small disturbance within me, and I expressed it in the abrupt manner mentioned by young Blake.

Roused thus from my reverie, I questioned the young fellow about his residence at Kalbsbraten, which has been always since the war a favorite place for our young gentry, and heard with some satisfaction that Potzdorff was married to the Behrenstein, Haabart had left the dragoons, the Crown Prince had broken with the —— but mum! of what interest are all these details to the reader, who has never been at friendly little Kalbsbraten?

Presently Lynch reaches me down one of the three books that formed his library (the "Racing Calendar" and a book of fishing-flies making up the remainder of the set). "And there's my album," says he. "You'll find plenty of hands in it that you'll recognize, as you are an old Pumpernickelaner." And so I did, in truth: it was a little book after the fashion of German albums, in which good simple little ledger every friend or acquaintance of the owner inscribes a poem or stanza from some favorite poet or philosopher with the transcriber's own name, as thus:—

"To the true house-friend, and beloved Irelandish youth.

"'Sera nunquam est ad bonos mores via.'

"WACKERBART, Professor at the Grand-Ducal Kalbsbraten-Pumpernickelisch Gymnasium."

Another writes,—

"'Wander on roses and forget me not.'

"AMALIA v. NACHTMUTZE,

"GEB. v. SHALAFROCK,"

with a flourish, and the picture mayhap of a rose. Let the reader imagine some hundreds of these interesting inscriptions, and he will have an idea of the book.

Turning over the leaves I came presently on DOROTHEA'S hand. There it was, the little neat, pretty handwriting, the dear old up-and-down strokes that I had not looked at for many a long year,—the Mediterranean heath, which grew on the sunniest banks of Fitz-Boodle's existence, and here found, dear, dear little sprig! in rude Galwagian bog-lands.

"Look at the other side of the page," says Lynch, rather sarcastically (for I don't care to confess that I kissed the name of "Dorothea v. Klingenspohr, born v. Speck" written under an extremely feeble passage of verse). "Look at the other side of the paper!"

I did, and what do you think I saw?

I saw the writing of five of the little Klingenspohrs, who have all sprung up since my time.

"Ha! ha! haw!" screamed the impertinent young Irishman, and the story was all over Connemara and Joyce's Country in a day after.

CHAPTER II

OTTILIA IN PARTICULAR

Some kind critic who peruses these writings will, doubtless, have the goodness to point out that the simile of the Mediterranean heath is applied to two personages in this chapter—to Ottilia and Dorothea, and say, Psha! the fellow is but a poor unimaginative creature not to be able to find a simile apiece at least for the girls; how much better would WE have done the business!

Well, it is a very pretty simile. The girls were rivals, were beautiful, I loved them both,—which should have the sprig of heath? Mr. Cruikshank (who has taken to serious painting) is getting ready for the exhibition a fine piece, representing Fitz-Boodle on the Urrisbeg Mountain, county Galway, Ireland, with a sprig of heath in his hand, hesitating, like Paris, on which of the beauties he should bestow it. In the background is a certain animal between two bundles of hay; but that I take to represent the critic, puzzled to which of my young beauties to assign the choice.

If Dorothea had been as rich as Miss Coutts, and had come to me the next day after the accident at the ball and said, "George, will you marry me?" it must not be supposed I would have done any such thing. THAT dream had vanished for ever: rage and pride took the place of love; and the only chance I had of recovering from my dreadful discomfiture was by bearing it bravely, and trying, if possible, to awaken a little compassion in my favor. I limped home (arranging my scheme with great presence of mind, as I actually sat spinning there on the ground)—I limped home, sent for Pflastersticken, the court-surgeon, and addressed him to the following effect: "Pflastersticken," says I, "there has been an accident at court of which you will hear. You will send in leeches, pills, and the deuce knows what, and you will say that I have dislocated my leg: for some days you will state that I am in considerable danger. You are a good fellow and a man of courage I know, for which very reason you can appreciate those qualities in another; so mind, if you breathe a word of my secret, either you or I must lose a life."

Away went the surgeon, and the next day all Kalbsbraten knew that I was on the point of death: I had been delirious all night, had had eighty leeches, besides I don't know how much medicine; but the Kalbsbrateners knew to a scruple. Whenever anybody was ill, this little kind society knew what medicines were prescribed. Everybody in the town knew what everybody had for dinner. If Madame Rumpel had her satin dyed ever so quietly, the whole society was on the qui vive; if Countess Pultuski sent to Berlin for a new set of teeth, not a person in Kalbsbraten but what was ready to compliment her as she put them on; if Potzdorff paid his tailor's bill, or Muffinstein bought a piece of black wax for his moustaches, it was the talk of the little city. And so, of course, was my accident. In their sorrow for my misfortune, Dorothea's was quite forgotten, and those eighty leeches saved me. I became interesting; I had cards left at my door; and I kept my room for a fortnight, during which time I read every one of M. Kotzebue's plays.

At the end of that period I was convalescent, though still a little lame. I called at old Speck's house and apologized for my clumsiness, with the most admirable coolness; I appeared at court, and stated calmly that I did not intend to dance any more; and when Klingenspohr grinned, I told that young gentleman such a piece of my mind as led to his wearing a large sticking-plaster patch on his nose: which was split as neatly down the middle as you would split an orange at dessert. In a word what man could do to repair my defeat, I did.

There is but one thing now of which I am ashamed—of those killing epigrams which I wrote (mon Dieu! must I own it?—but even the fury of my anger proves the extent of my love!) against the Speck family. They were handed about in confidence at court, and made a frightful sensation:

"IS IT POSSIBLE?"

"There happened at Schloss P-mp-rn-ckel,
 A strange mishap our sides to tickle,
 And set the people in a roar;—
 A strange caprice of Fortune fickle:
 I never thought at Pumpernickel
 To see a SPECK UPON THE FLOOR!"

LA PERFIDE ALBION; OR, A CAUTION TO WALTZERS.

"'Come to the dance,' the Briton said,
And forward D-r-th-a led,

Fair, fresh, and three-and-twenty!
Ah, girls; beware of Britons red!
  What wonder that it TURNED HER HEAD?
SAT VERBUM SAPIENTI."

"REASONS FOR NOT MARRYING.

"'The lovely Miss S.
 Will surely say "yes,"
  You've only to ask and try;'
 'That subject we'll quit;'
Says Georgy the wit,
  'I'VE A MUCH BETTER SPEC IN MY EYE!'"

This last epigram especially was voted so killing that it flew like wildfire; and I know for a fact that our Charge-d'Affaires at Kalbsbraten sent a courier express with it to the Foreign Office in England, whence, through our amiable Foreign Secretary, Lord P-lm-rston, it made its way into every fashionable circle: nay, I have reason to believe caused a smile on the cheek of R-y-lty itself. Now that Time has taken away the sting of these epigrams, there can be no harm in giving them; and 'twas well enough then to endeavor to hide under the lash of wit the bitter pangs of humiliation: but my heart bleeds now to think that I should have ever brought a tear on the gentle cheek of Dorothea.

Not content with this—with humiliating her by satire, and with wounding her accepted lover across the nose—I determined to carry my revenge still farther, and to fall in love with somebody else. This person was Ottilia v. Schlippenschlopp.

Otho Sigismund Freyherr von Schlippenschlopp, Knight Grand Cross of the Ducal Order of the Two-Necked Swan of Pumpernickel, of the Porc-et-Siflet of Kalbsbraten, Commander of the George and Blue-Boar of Dummerland, Excellency, and High Chancellor of the United Duchies, lived in the second floor of a house in the Schwapsgasse; where, with his private income and his revenues as Chancellor, amounting together to some 300L. per annum, he maintained such a state as very few other officers of the Grand-Ducal Crown could exhibit. The Baron is married to Marie Antoinette, a Countess of the house of Kartoffelstadt, branches of which have taken root all over Germany. He has no sons, and but one daughter, the Fraulein OTTILIA.

The Chancellor is a worthy old gentleman, too fat and wheezy to preside at the Privy Council, fond of his pipe, his ease, and his rubber. His lady is a very tall and pale Roman-nosed Countess, who looks as gentle as Mrs. Robert Roy, where, in the novel, she is for putting Baillie Nicol Jarvie into the lake, and who keeps the honest Chancellor in the greatest order. The Fraulein Ottilia had not arrived at Kalbsbraten when the little affair between me and Dorothea was going on; or rather had only just come in for the conclusion of it, being presented for the first time that year at the ball where I—where I met with my accident.

At the time when the Countess was young, it was not the fashion in her country to educate the young ladies so highly as since they have been educated; and provided they could waltz, sew, and make puddings, they were thought to be decently bred; being seldom called upon for algebra or Sanscrit in the discharge of the honest duties of their lives. But Fraulein Ottilia was of the modern school in this respect, and came back from the pension at Strasburg speaking all the languages, dabbling in all the sciences: an historian, a poet,—a blue of the ultramarinest sort, in a word. What a difference there was, for instance, between poor, simple Dorothea's love of novel reading and the profound encyclopaedic learning of Ottilia!

Before the latter arrived from Strasburg (where she had been under the care of her aunt the canoness, Countess Ottilia of Kartoffeldstadt, to whom I here beg to offer my humblest respects), Dorothea had passed for a bel esprit in the little court circle, and her little simple stock of accomplishments had amused us all very well. She used to sing "Herz, mein Herz" and "T'en souviens-tu," in a decent manner (ONCE, before heaven, I thought her singing better than Grisi's), and then she had a little album in which she drew flowers, and used to embroider slippers wonderfully, and was very merry at a game of loto or forfeits, and had a hundred small agremens de societe! which rendered her an acceptable member of it.

But when Ottilia arrived, poor Dolly's reputation was crushed in a month. The former wrote poems both in French and German; she painted landscapes and portraits in real oil; and she twanged off a rattling piece of Listz or Kalkbrenner in such a brilliant way, that Dora scarcely dared to touch the instrument after her, or ventured, after Ottilia had trilled and gurgled through "Una voce," or "Di piacer" (Rossini was in fashion then), to lift up her little modest pipe in a ballad. What was the use of the poor thing going to sit in the park, where so many of the young officers used ever to gather round her? Whir! Ottilia went by galloping on a chestnut mare with a groom after her, and presently all the young fellows who could buy or hire horseflesh were prancing in her train.

When they met, Ottilia would bounce towards her soul's darling, and put her hands round her waist, and call her by a thousand affectionate names, and then talk of her as only ladies or authors can talk of one another. How tenderly she would hint at Dora's little imperfections of education!—how cleverly she would insinuate that the poor girl had no wit! and, thank God, no more she had. The fact is, that do what I will I see I'm in love with her still, and would be if she had fifty children; but my passion blinded me THEN, and every arrow that fiery Ottilia discharged I marked with savage joy. Dolly, thank heaven, didn't mind the wit much; she was too simple for that. But still the recurrence of it would leave in her heart a vague, indefinite feeling of pain, and somehow she began to understand that her empire was passing away, and that her dear friend hated her like poison; and so she married Klingenspohr. I have written myself almost into a reconciliation with the silly fellow; for the truth is, he has been a good, honest husband to her, and she has children, and makes puddings, and is happy.

Ottilia was pale and delicate. She wore her glistening black hair in bands, and dressed in vapory white muslin. She sang her own words to her harp, and they commonly insinuated that she was alone in the world,—that she suffered some inexpressible and mysterious heart-pangs, the lot of all finer geniuses,— that though she lived and moved in the world she was not of it, that she was of a consumptive tendency and might look for a premature interment. She even had fixed on the spot where she should lie: the violets grew there, she said, the river went moaning by; the gray willow whispered sadly over her head, and her heart pined to be at rest. "Mother," she would say, turning to her parent, "promise me— promise me to lay me in that spot when the parting hour has come!" At which Madame de Schlippenschlopp would shriek, and grasp her in her arms; and at which, I confess, I would myself blubber like a child. She had six darling friends at school, and every courier from Kalbsbraten carried off whole reams of her letter-paper.

In Kalbsbraten, as in every other German town, there are a vast number of literary characters, of whom our young friend quickly became the chief. They set up a literary journal, which appeared once a week, upon light-blue or primrose paper, and which, in compliment to the lovely Ottilia's maternal name, was called the Kartoffelnkranz. Here are a couple of her ballads extracted from the Kranz, and by far the most cheerful specimen of her style. For in her songs she never would willingly let off the heroines without a suicide or a consumption. She never would hear of such a thing as a happy marriage, and had an appetite for grief quite amazing in so young a person. As for her dying and desiring to be buried under the willow-tree, of which the first ballad is the subject, though I believed the story then, I have at present some doubts about it. For, since the publication of my Memoirs, I have been thrown much into the society of literary persons (who admire my style hugely), and egad! though some of them are dismal enough in their works, I find them in their persons the least sentimental class that ever a gentleman fell in with.

"THE WILLOW-TREE.

"Know ye the willow-tree
 Whose gray leaves quiver,
  Whispering gloomily
To yon pale river?
Lady, at even-tide
 Wander not near it,
They say its branches hide
A sad, lost spirit!

"Once to the willow-tree
 A maid came fearful,
Pale seemed her cheek to be,
Her blue eye tearful;
Soon as she saw the tree,
 Her step moved fleeter,
 No one was there—ah me!
No one to meet her!

"Quick beat her heart to hear
 The far bell's chime
Toll from the chapel-tower
 The trysting time:
But the red sun went down
 In golden flame,
 And though she looked round,
 Yet no one came!

"Presently came the night,
 Sadly to greet her,—
Moon in her silver light,
 Stars in their glitter.
 Then sank the moon away
 Under the billow,
Still wept the maid alone—
 There by the willow!

"Through the long darkness,
 By the stream rolling,
  Hour after hour went on
Tolling and tolling.
  Long was the darkness,
  Lonely and stilly;
  Shrill came the night-wind,
Piercing and chilly.

"Shrill blew the morning breeze,
 Biting and cold,
Bleak peers the gray dawn
Over the wold.
 Bleak over moor and stream
 Looks the grey dawn,
  Gray, with dishevelled hair,
  Still stands the willow there—

THE MAID IS GONE!

"Domine, Domine! Sing we a litany,— Sing for poor maiden-hearts broken and weary; Domine, Domine!
Sing we a litany, wail we and weep we a wild Miserere!"

One of the chief beauties of this ballad (for the translation of which I received some well-merited
compliments) is the delicate way in which the suicide of the poor young woman under the willow-tree is
hinted at; for that she threw herself into the water and became one among the lilies of the stream, is as
clear as a pikestaff. Her suicide is committed some time in the darkness, when the slow hours move on
tolling and tolling, and is hinted at darkly as befits the time and the deed.

But that unromantic brute, Van Cutsem, the Dutch Charge-d'Affaires, sent to the Kartoffelnkranz of the
week after a conclusion of the ballad, which shows what a poor creature he must be. His pretext for
writing it was, he said, because he could not bear such melancholy endings to poems and young women,
and therefore he submitted the following lines:—

I

"Long by the willow-trees
  Vainly they sought her,
Wild rang the mother's screams
  O'er the gray water:
  'Where is my lovely one?
  Where is my daughter?

II

"'Rouse thee, sir constable—
 Rouse thee and look;

Fisherman, bring your net,
  Boatman your hook.
  Beat in the lily-beds,
  Dive in the brook!'

III

"Vainly the constable
  Shouted and called her;
Vainly the fisherman
    Beat the green alder;
  Vainly he flung the net,
  Never it hauled her!

IV

"Mother beside the fire
  Sat, her nightcap in;
Father, in easy chair,
  Gloomily napping;
  When at the window-sill
  Came a light tapping!

V

"And a pale countenance
  Looked through the casement.
    Loud beat the mother's heart,
  Sick with amazement,
And at the vision which
  Came to surprise her,
  Shrieked in an agony—
  'Lor! it's Elizar!'

VI

"Yes, 'twas Elizabeth—
  Yes, 'twas their girl;
Pale was her cheek, and her
Hair out of curl.
  'Mother!' the loving one,
  Blushing, exclaimed,   'Let not your innocent
  Lizzy be blamed.

VII

"'Yesterday, going to aunt
  Jones's to tea,
Mother, dear mother, I
FORGOT THE DOOR-KEY!
  And as the night was cold,
And the way steep,
  Mrs. Jones kept me to
  Breakfast and sleep.'

VIII

"Whether her Pa and Ma
  Fully believed her,
That we shall never know,
Stern they received her;
  And for the work of that
Cruel, though short, night,
  Sent her to bed without
  Tea for a fortnight.

IX

"MORAL

"Hey diddle diddlety,
  Cat and the Fiddlety,
Maidens of England take caution by she!
  Let love and suicide
  Never tempt you aside,
  And always remember to take the door-key!"

Some people laughed at this parody, and even preferred it to the original; but for myself I have no patience with the individual who can turn the finest sentiments of our nature into ridicule, and make everything sacred a subject of scorn. The next ballad is less gloomy than that of the willow-tree, and in it the lovely writer expresses her longing for what has charmed us all, and, as it were, squeezes the whole spirit of the fairy tale into a few stanzas:—

"FAIRY DAYS.

"Beside the old hall-fire—upon my nurse's knee,
  Of happy fairy days—what tales were told to me!
  I thought the world was once—all peopled with princesses,
  And my heart would beat to hear—their loves and their distresses;

And many a quiet night,—in slumber sweet and deep,
The pretty fairy people—would visit me in sleep.

"I saw them in my dreams—come flying east and west,
With wondrous fairy gifts—the new-born babe they bless'd;
One has brought a jewel—and one a crown of gold,
And one has brought a curse—but she is wrinkled and old.
The gentle queen turns pale—to hear those words of sin,
But the king he only laughs—and bids the dance begin.

"The babe has grown to be—the fairest of the land
And rides the forest green—a hawk upon her hand.
An ambling palfrey white—a golden robe and crown;
I've seen her in my dreams—riding up and down;
And heard the ogre laugh—as she fell into his snare,
At the little tender creature—who wept and tore her hair!

"But ever when it seemed—her need was at the sorest
A prince in shining mail—comes prancing through the forest.
A waving ostrich-plume—a buckler burnished bright;
I've seen him in my dreams—good sooth! a gallant knight.
His lips are coral red—beneath a dark moustache;
See how he waves his hand—and how his blue eyes flash!

"'Come forth, thou Paynim knight!'—he shouts in accents clear.
The giant and the maid—both tremble his voice to hear.
Saint Mary guard him well!—he draws his falchion keen,
The giant and the knight—are fighting on the green.
I see them in my dreams—his blade gives stroke on stroke,
The giant pants and reels—and tumbles like an oak!

"With what a blushing grace—he falls upon his knee
And takes the lady's hand—and whispers, 'You are free!'
Ah! happy childish tales—of knight and faerie!
I waken from my dreams—but there's ne'er a knight for me;
I waken from my dreams—and wish that I could be
A child by the old hall-fire—upon my nurse's knee."

Indeed, Ottilia looked like a fairy herself: pale, small, slim, and airy. You could not see her face, as it
were, for her eyes, which were so wild, and so tender, and shone so that they would have dazzled an
eagle, much more a poor goose of a Fitz-Boodle. In the theatre, when she sat on the opposite side of the
house, those big eyes used to pursue me as I sat pretending to listen to the "Zauberflote," or to "Don
Carlos," or "Egmont," and at the tender passages, especially, they would have such a winning, weeping,
imploring look with them as flesh and blood could not bear.

Shall I tell how I became a poet for the dear girl's sake? 'Tis surely unnecessary after the reader has
perused the above versions of her poems. Shall I tell what wild follies I committed in prose as well as in
verse? how I used to watch under her window of icy evenings, and with chilblainy fingers sing serenades

to her on the guitar? Shall I tell how, in a sledging-party, I had the happiness to drive her, and of the delightful privilege which is, on these occasions, accorded to the driver?

Any reader who has spent a winter in Germany perhaps knows it. A large party of a score or more of sledges is formed. Away they go to some pleasure-house that has been previously fixed upon, where a ball and collation are prepared, and where each man, as his partner descends, has the delicious privilege of saluting her. O heavens and earth! I may grow to be a thousand years old, but I can never forget the rapture of that salute.

"The keen air has given me an appetite," said the dear angel, as we entered the supper-room; and to say the truth, fairy as she was, she made a remarkably good meal—consuming a couple of basins of white soup, several kinds of German sausages, some Westphalia ham, some white puddings, an anchovy-salad made with cornichons and onions, sweets innumerable, and a considerable quantity of old Steinwein and rum-punch afterwards. Then she got up and danced as brisk as a fairy; in which operation I of course did not follow her, but had the honor, at the close of the evening's amusement, once more to have her by my side in the sledge, as we swept in the moonlight over the snow.

Kalbsbraten is a very hospitable place as far as tea-parties are concerned, but I never was in one where dinners were so scarce. At the palace they occurred twice or thrice in a month; but on these occasions spinsters were not invited, and I seldom had the opportunity of seeing my Ottilia except at evening-parties.

Nor are these, if the truth must be told, very much to my taste. Dancing I have forsworn, whist is too severe a study for me, and I do not like to play ecarte with old ladies, who are sure to cheat you in the course of an evening's play.

But to have an occasional glance at Ottilia was enough; and many and many a napoleon did I lose to her mamma, Madame de Schlippenschlopp, for the blest privilege of looking at her daughter. Many is the tea-party I went to, shivering into cold clothes after dinner (which is my abomination) in order to have one little look at the lady of my soul.

At these parties there were generally refreshments of a nature more substantial than mere tea punch, both milk and rum, hot wine, consomme, and a peculiar and exceedingly disagreeable sandwich made of a mixture of cold white puddings and garlic, of which I have forgotten the name, and always detested the savor.

Gradually a conviction came upon me that Ottilia ATE A GREAT DEAL.

I do not dislike to see a woman eat comfortably. I even think that an agreeable woman ought to be friande, and should love certain little dishes and knick-knacks. I know that though at dinner they commonly take nothing, they have had roast-mutton with the children at two, and laugh at their pretensions to starvation.

No! a woman who eats a grain of rice, like Amina in the "Arabian Nights," is absurd and unnatural; but there is a modus in rebus: there is no reason why she should be a ghoul, a monster, an ogress, a horrid gormandizeress—faugh!

It was, then, with a rage amounting almost to agony, that I found Ottilia ate too much at every meal. She was always eating, and always eating too much. If I went there in the morning, there was the horrid familiar odor of those oniony sandwiches; if in the afternoon, dinner had been just removed, and I was choked by reeking reminiscences of roast-meat. Tea we have spoken of. She gobbled up more cakes than any six people present; then came the supper and the sandwiches again, and the egg-flip and the horrible rum-punch.

She was as thin as ever—paler if possible than ever:—but, by heavens! HER NOSE BEGAN TO GROW RED!

Mon Dieu! how I used to watch and watch it! Some days it was purple, some days had more of the vermilion—I could take an affidavit that after a heavy night's supper it was more swollen, more red than before.

I recollect one night when we were playing a round game (I had been looking at her nose very eagerly and sadly for some time), she of herself brought up the conversation about eating, and confessed that she had five meals a day.

"THAT ACCOUNTS FOR IT!" says I, flinging down the cards, and springing up and rushing like a madman out of the room. I rushed away into the night, and wrestled with my passion. "What! Marry," said I, "a woman who eats meat twenty-one times in a week, besides breakfast and tea? Marry a sarcophagus, a cannibal, a butcher's shop?—Away!" I strove and strove. I drank, I groaned, I wrestled and fought with my love—but it overcame me: one look of those eyes brought me to her feet again. I yielded myself up like a slave; I fawned and whined for her; I thought her nose was not so VERY red.

Things came to this pitch that I sounded his Highness's Minister to know whether he would give me service in the Duchy; I thought of purchasing an estate there. I was given to understand that I should get a chamberlain's key and some post of honor did I choose to remain, and I even wrote home to my brother Tom in England, hinting a change in my condition.

At this juncture the town of Hamburg sent his Highness the Grand Duke (apropos of a commercial union which was pending between the two States) a singular present: no less than a certain number of barrels of oysters, which are considered extreme luxuries in Germany, especially in the inland parts of the country, where they are almost unknown.

In honor of the oysters and the new commercial treaty (which arrived in fourgons despatched for the purpose), his Highness announced a grand supper and ball, and invited all the quality of all the principalities round about. It was a splendid affair: the grand saloon brilliant with hundreds of uniforms and brilliant toilettes—not the least beautiful among them, I need not say, was Ottilia.

At midnight the supper-rooms were thrown open and we formed into little parties of six, each having a table, nobly served with plate, a lackey in attendance, and a gratifying ice-pail or two of champagne to egayer the supper. It was no small cost to serve five hundred people on silver, and the repast was certainly a princely and magnificent one.

I had, of course, arranged with Mademoiselle de Schlippenschlopp. Captains Frumpel and Fridelberger of the Duke's Guard, Mesdames de Butterbrod and Bopp, formed our little party.

The first course, of course, consisted of THE OYSTERS. Ottilia's eyes gleamed with double brilliancy as the lackey opened them. There were nine apiece for us—how well I recollect the number!

I never was much of an oyster-eater, nor can I relish them in naturalibus as some do, but require a quantity of sauces, lemons, cayenne peppers, bread and butter, and so forth, to render them palatable.

By the time I had made my preparations, Ottilia, the Captains, and the two ladies, had wellnigh finished theirs. Indeed Ottilia had gobbled up all hers, and there were only my nine in the dish.

I took one—IT WAS BAD. The scent of it was enough,—they were all bad. Ottilia had eaten nine bad oysters.

I put down the horrid shell. Her eyes glistened more and more; she could not take them off the tray.

"Dear Herr George," she said, "WILL YOU GIVE ME YOUR OYSTERS?"

She had them all down—before—I could say—Jack—Robinson!

I left Kalbsbraten that night, and have never been there since.

FITZ-BOODLE'S PROFESSIONS

BEING APPEALS TO THE UNEMPLOYED YOUNGER SONS OF THE NOBILITY.

FIRST PROFESSION

The fair and honest proposition in which I offered to communicate privately with parents and guardians, relative to two new and lucrative professions which I had discovered, has, I find from the publisher, elicited not one single inquiry from those personages, who I can't but think are very little careful of their children's welfare to allow such a chance to be thrown away. It is not for myself I speak, as my conscience proudly tells me; for though I actually gave up Ascot in order to be in the way should any father of a family be inclined to treat with me regarding my discoveries, yet I am grieved, not on my own account, but on theirs, and for the wretched penny-wise policy that has held them back.

That they must feel an interest in my announcement is unquestionable. Look at the way in which the public prints of all parties have noticed my appearance in the character of a literary man! Putting aside my personal narrative, look at the offer I made to the nation,—a choice of no less than two new professions! Suppose I had invented as many new kinds of butcher's meat; does any one pretend that the world, tired as it is of the perpetual recurrence of beef, mutton, veal, cold beef, cold veal, cold mutton, hashed ditto, would not have jumped eagerly at the delightful intelligence that their old, stale, stupid meals were about to be varied at last?

Of course people would have come forward. I should have had deputations from Mr. Gibletts and the fashionable butchers of this world; petitions would have poured in from Whitechapel salesmen; the speculators panting to know the discovery; the cautious with stock in hand eager to bribe me to silence and prevent the certain depreciation of the goods which they already possessed. I should have dealt with them, not greedily or rapaciously, but on honest principles of fair barter. "Gentlemen," I should have said, or rather, "Gents"—which affectionate diminutive is, I am given to understand, at present much in use among commercial persons—"Gents, my researches, my genius, or my good fortune, have brought me to the valuable discovery about which you are come to treat. Will you purchase it outright, or will you give the discoverer an honest share of the profits resulting from your speculation? My position in the world puts ME out of the power of executing the vast plan I have formed, but 'twill be a certain fortune to him who engages in it; and why should not I, too, participate in that fortune?"

Such would have been my manner of dealing with the world, too, with regard to my discovery of the new professions. Does not the world want new professions? Are there not thousands of well-educated men panting, struggling, pushing, starving, in the old ones? Grim tenants of chambers looking out for attorneys who never come?—wretched physicians practising the stale joke of being called out of church until people no longer think fit even to laugh or to pity? Are there not hoary-headed midshipmen, antique ensigns growing mouldy upon fifty years' half-pay? Nay, are there not men who would pay anything to be employed rather than remain idle? But such is the glut of professionals, the horrible cut-throat competition among them, that there is no chance for one in a thousand, be he ever so willing, or brave, or clever: in the great ocean of life he makes a few strokes, and puffs, and sputters, and sinks, and the innumerable waves overwhelm him and he is heard of no more.

Walking to my banker's t'other day—and I pledge my sacred honor this story is true—I met a young fellow whom I had known attache to an embassy abroad, a young man of tolerable parts, unwearied patience, with some fortune too, and, moreover, allied to a noble Whig family, whose interest had procured him his appointment to the legation at Krahwinkel, where I knew him. He remained for ten years a diplomatic character; he was the working-man of the legation; he sent over the most diffuse translations of the German papers for the use of the Foreign Secretary; he signed passports with most astonishing ardor; he exiled himself for ten long years in a wretched German town, dancing attendance at court-balls and paying no end of money for uniforms. And what for? At the end of the ten years—during which period of labor he never received a single shilling from the Government which employed him (rascally spendthrift of a Government, va!),—he was offered the paid attacheship to the court of H. M. the King of the Mosquito Islands, and refused that appointment a week before the Whig Ministry retired. Then he knew that there was no further chance for him, and incontinently quitted the diplomatic service for ever, and I have no doubt will sell his uniform a bargain. The Government had HIM a bargain certainly; nor is he by any means the first person who has been sold at that price.

Well, my worthy friend met me in the street and informed me of these facts with a smiling countenance,—which I thought a masterpiece of diplomacy. Fortune had been belaboring and kicking him for ten whole years, and here he was grinning in my face: could Monsieur de Talleyrand have acted better? "I have given up diplomacy," said Protocol, quite simply and good-humoredly, "for between you and me, my good fellow, it's a very slow profession; sure, perhaps, but slow. But though I gained no actual pecuniary remuneration in the service, I have learned all the languages in Europe, which will be invaluable to me in my new profession—the mercantile one—in which directly I looked out for a post I found one."

"What! and a good pay?" said I.

"Why, no; that's absurd, you know. No young men, strangers to business, are paid much to speak of. Besides, I don't look to a paltry clerk's pay. Some day, when thoroughly acquainted with the business (I shall learn it in about seven years), I shall go into a good house with my capital and become junior partner."

"And meanwhile?"

"Meanwhile I conduct the foreign correspondence of the eminent house of Jam, Ram, and Johnson; and very heavy it is, I can tell you. From nine till six every day, except foreign post days, and then from nine till eleven. Dirty dark court to sit in; snobs to talk to,—great change, as you may fancy."

"And you do all this for nothing?"

"I do it to learn the business." And so saying Protocol gave me a knowing nod and went his way.

Good heavens! I thought, and is this a true story? Are there hundreds of young men in a similar situation at the present day, giving away the best years of their youth for the sake of a mere windy hope of something in old age, and dying before they come to the goal? In seven years he hopes to have a business, and then to have the pleasure of risking his money? He will be admitted into some great house as a particular favor, and three months after the house will fail. Has it not happened to a thousand of our acquaintance? I thought I would run after him and tell him about the new professions that I have invented.

"Oh! ay! those you wrote about in Fraser's Magazine. Egad! George, Necessity makes strange fellows of us all. Who would ever have thought of you SPELLING, much more writing?"

"Never mind that. Will you, if I tell you of a new profession that, with a little cleverness and instruction from me, you may bring to a most successful end—will you, I say, make me a fair return?"

"My dear creature," replied young Protocol, "what nonsense you talk! I saw that very humbug in the Magazine. You say you have made a great discovery—very good; you puff your discovery—very right; you ask money for it—nothing can be more reasonable; and then you say that you intend to make your discovery public in the next number of the Magazine. Do you think I will be such a fool as to give you money for a thing which I can have next month for nothing? Good-by, George my boy; the NEXT discovery you make I'll tell you how to get a better price for it." And with this the fellow walked off, looking supremely knowing and clever.

This tale of the person I have called Protocol is not told without a purpose, you may be sure. In the first place, it shows what are the reasons that nobody has made application to me concerning the new professions, namely, because I have passed my word to make them known in this Magazine, which persons may have for the purchasing, stealing, borrowing, or hiring, and, therefore, they will never think of applying personally to me. And, secondly, his story proves also my assertion, viz, that all professions are most cruelly crowded at present, and that men will make the most absurd outlay and sacrifices for the smallest chance of success at some future period. Well, then, I will be a benefactor to my race, if I cannot be to one single member of it, whom I love better than most men. What I have discovered I will make known; there shall be no shilly-shallying work here, no circumlocution, no bottle-conjuring business. But oh! I wish for all our sakes that I had had an opportunity to impart the secret to one or two persons only; for, after all, but one or two can live in the manner I would suggest. And when the discovery is made known, I am sure ten thousand will try. The rascals! I can see their brass-plates gleaming over scores of doors. Competition will ruin my professions, as it has all others.

It must be premised that the two professions are intended for gentlemen, and gentlemen only—men of birth and education. No others could support the parts which they will be called upon to play.

And, likewise, it must be honestly confessed that these professions have, to a certain degree, been exercised before. Do not cry out at this and say it is no discovery! I say it IS a discovery. It is a discovery if I show you—a gentleman—a profession which you may exercise without derogation, or loss of standing, with certain profit, nay, possibly with honor, and of which, until the reading of this present page, you never thought but as of a calling beneath your rank and quite below your reach. Sir, I do not mean to say that I create a profession. I cannot create gold; but if, when discovered, I find the means of putting it in your pocket, do I or do I not deserve credit?

I see you sneer contemptuously when I mention to you the word AUCTIONEER. "Is this all," you say, "that this fellow brags and prates about? An auctioneer forsooth! he might as well have 'invented' chimney-sweeping!"

No such thing. A little boy of seven, be he ever so low of birth, can do this as well as you. Do you suppose that little stolen Master Montague made a better sweeper than the lowest-bred chummy that yearly commemorates his release? No, sir. And he might have been ever so much a genius or gentleman, and not have been able to make his trade respectable.

But all such trades as can be rendered decent the aristocracy has adopted one by one. At first they followed the profession of arms, flouting all others as unworthy, and thinking it ungentlemanlike to know how to read or write. They did not go into the church in very early days, till the money to be got from the church was strong enough to tempt them. It is but of later years that they have condescended to go to the bar, and since the same time only that we see some of them following trades. I know an English lord's son, who is, or was, a wine-merchant (he may have been a bankrupt for what I know). As for bankers, several partners in banking-houses have four balls to their coronets, and I have no doubt that another sort of banking, viz, that practised by gentlemen who lend small sums of money upon deposited securities, will be one day followed by the noble order, so that they may have four balls on their coronets and carriages, and three in front of their shops.

Yes, the nobles come peoplewards as the people, on the other hand, rise and mingle with the nobles. With the plebs, of course, Fitz-Boodle, in whose veins flows the blood of a thousand kings, can have nothing to do; but, watching the progress of the world, 'tis impossible to deny that the good old days of our race are passed away. We want money still as much as ever we did; but we cannot go down from our castles with horse and sword and waylay fat merchants—no, no, confounded new policemen and the assize-courts prevent that. Younger brothers cannot be pages to noble houses, as of old they were, serving gentle dames without disgrace, handing my lord's rose-water to wash, or holding his stirrup as he mounted for the chase. A page, forsooth! A pretty figure would George Fitz-Boodle or any other man of fashion cut, in a jacket covered with sugar-loafed buttons, and handing in penny-post notes on a silver tray. The plebs have robbed us of THAT trade among others: nor, I confess, do I much grudge them their trouvaille. Neither can we collect together a few scores of free lances, like honest Hugh Calverly in the Black Prince's time, or brave Harry Butler of Wallenstein's dragoons, and serve this or that prince, Peter the Cruel or Henry of Trastamare, Gustavus or the Emperor, at our leisure; or, in default of service, fight and rob on our own gallant account, as the good gentlemen of old did. Alas! no. In South America or Texas, perhaps, a man might have a chance that way; but in the ancient world no man can fight except in the king's service (and a mighty bad service that is too), and the lowest European sovereign, were it Baldomero Espartero himself, would think nothing of seizing the best-born condottiere that ever drew sword, and shooting him down like the vulgarest deserter.

What, then, is to be done? We must discover fresh fields of enterprise—of peaceable and commercial enterprise in a peaceful and commercial age. I say, then, that the auctioneer's pulpit has never yet been ascended by a scion of the aristocracy, and am prepared to prove that they might scale it, and do so with dignity and profit.

For the auctioneer's pulpit is just the peculiar place where a man of social refinement, of elegant wit, of polite perceptions, can bring his wit, his eloquence, his taste, and his experience of life, most delightfully into play. It is not like the bar, where the better and higher qualities of a man of fashion find no room for exercise. In defending John Jorrocks in an action of trespass, for cutting down a stick in Sam Snooks's field, what powers of mind do you require?—powers of mind, that is, which Mr. Serjeant Snorter, a butcher's son with a great loud voice, a sizar at Cambridge, a wrangler, and so forth, does not possess as well as yourself? Snorter has never been in decent society in his life. He thinks the bar-mess the most fashionable assemblage in Europe, and the jokes of "grand day" the ne plus ultra of wit. Snorter lives near Russell Square, eats beef and Yorkshire-pudding, is a judge of port-wine, is in all social respects your inferior. Well, it is ten to one but in the case of Snooks v. Jorrocks, before mentioned, he will be a better advocate than you; he knows the law of the case entirely, and better probably than you. He can speak long, loud, to the point, grammatically—more grammatically than you, no doubt, will condescend to do. In the case of Snooks v. Jorrocks he is all that can be desired. And so about dry disputes, respecting real property, he knows the law; and, beyond this, has no more need to be a gentleman than my body-servant has—who, by the way, from constant intercourse with the best society, IS almost a gentleman. But this is apart from the question.

Now, in the matter of auctioneering, this, I apprehend, is not the case, and I assert that a high-bred gentleman, with good powers of mind and speech, must, in such a profession, make a fortune. I do not mean in all auctioneering matters. I do not mean that such a person should be called upon to sell the good-will of a public-house, or discourse about the value of the beer-barrels, or bars with pewter fittings, or the beauty of a trade doing a stroke of so many hogsheads a week. I do not ask a gentleman to go down and sell pigs, ploughs, and cart-horses, at Stoke Pogis; or to enlarge at the Auction-Rooms, Wapping, upon the beauty of the "Lively Sally" schooner. These articles of commerce or use can be better appreciated by persons in a different rank of life to his.

But there are a thousand cases in which a gentleman only can do justice to the sale of objects which the necessity or convenience of the genteel world may require to change hands. All articles properly called of taste should be put under his charge. Pictures,—he is a travelled man, has seen and judged the best galleries of Europe, and can speak of them as a common person cannot. For, mark you, you must have the confidence of your society, you must be able to be familiar with them, to plant a happy mot in a graceful manner, to appeal to my lord or the duchess in such a modest, easy, pleasant way as that her grace should not be hurt by your allusion to her—nay, amused (like the rest of the company) by the manner in which it was done.

What is more disgusting than the familiarity of a snob? What more loathsome than the swaggering quackery of some present holders of the hammer? There was a late sale, for instance, which made some noise in the world (I mean the late Lord Gimcrack's, at Dilberry Hill). Ah! what an opportunity was lost there! I declare solemnly that I believe, but for the absurd quackery and braggadocio of the advertisements, much more money would have been bid; people were kept away by the vulgar trumpeting of the auctioneer, and could not help thinking the things were worthless that were so outrageously lauded.

They say that sort of Bartholomew-fair advocacy (in which people are invited to an entertainment by the medium of a hoarse yelling beef-eater, twenty-four drums, and a jack-pudding turning head over heels) is absolutely necessary to excite the public attention. What an error! I say that the refined individual so accosted is more likely to close his ears, and, shuddering, run away from the booth. Poor Horace Waddlepoodle! to think that thy gentle accumulation of bricabrac should have passed away in such a manner! by means of a man who brings down a butterfly with a blunderbuss, and talks of a pin's head through a speaking-trumpet! Why, the auctioneer's very voice was enough to crack the Sevres porcelain and blow the lace into annihilation. Let it be remembered that I speak of the gentleman in his public character merely, meaning to insinuate nothing more than I would by stating that Lord Brougham speaks with a northern accent, or that the voice of Mr. Shell is sometimes unpleasantly shrill.

Now the character I have formed to myself of a great auctioneer is this. I fancy him a man of first-rate and irreproachable birth and fashion. I fancy his person so agreeable that it must be a pleasure for ladies to behold and tailors to dress it. As a private man he must move in the very best society, which will flock round his pulpit when he mounts it in his public calling. It will be a privilege for vulgar people to attend the hall where he lectures; and they will consider it an honor to be allowed to pay their money for articles the value of which is stamped by his high recommendation. Nor can such a person be a mere fribble; nor can any loose hanger-on of fashion imagine he may assume the character. The gentleman auctioneer must be an artist above all, adoring his profession; and adoring it, what must he not know? He must have a good knowledge of the history and language of all nations; not the knowledge of the mere critical scholar, but of the lively and elegant man of the world. He will not commit the gross blunders of pronunciation that untravelled Englishmen perpetrate; he will not degrade his subject by coarse eulogy or sicken his audience with vulgar banter. He will know where to apply praise and wit properly; he will have the tact only acquired in good society, and know where a joke is in place, and how far a compliment may go. He will not outrageously and indiscriminately laud all objects committed to his charge, for he knows the value of praise; that diamonds, could we have them by the bushel, would be used as coals; that above all, he has a character of sincerity to support; that he is not merely the advocate of the person who employs him, but that the public is his client too, who honors him and confides in him. Ask him to sell a copy of Raffaelle for an original; a trumpery modern Brussels counterfeit for real old Mechlin; some common French forged crockery for the old delightful, delicate, Dresden china; and he will quit you with scorn, or order his servant to show you the door of his study.

Study, by the way,—no, "study" is a vulgar word; every word is vulgar which a man uses to give the world an exaggerated notion of himself or his condition. When the wretched bagman, brought up to give evidence before Judge Coltman, was asked what his trade was, and replied that "he represented the house of Dobson and Hobson," he showed himself to be a vulgar, mean-souled wretch, and was most properly reprimanded by his lordship. To be a bagman is to be humble, but not of necessity vulgar. Pomposity is vulgar, to ape a higher rank than your own is vulgar, for an ensign of militia to call himself captain is vulgar, or for a bagman to style himself the "representative" of Dobson and Hobson. The honest auctioneer, then, will not call his room his study; but his "private room," or his office, or whatever may be the phrase commonly used among auctioneers.

He will not for the same reason call himself (as once in a momentary feeling of pride and enthusiasm for the profession I thought he should)—he will not call himself an "advocate," but an auctioneer. There is no need to attempt to awe people by big titles: let each man bear his own name without shame. And a very gentlemanlike and agreeable, though exceptional position (for it is clear that there cannot be more than two of the class,) may the auctioneer occupy.

He must not sacrifice his honesty, then, either for his own sake or his clients', in any way, nor tell fibs about himself or them. He is by no means called upon to draw the long bow in their behalf; all that his office obliges him to do—and let us hope his disposition will lead him to do it also—is to take a favorable, kindly, philanthropic view of the world; to say what can fairly be said by a good-natured and ingenious man in praise of any article for which he is desirous to awaken public sympathy. And how readily and pleasantly may this be done! I will take upon myself, for instance, to write an eulogium upon So-and-So's last novel, which shall be every word of it true; and which work, though to some discontented spirits it might appear dull, may be shown to be really amusing and instructive,—nay, IS amusing and instructive,—to those who have the art of discovering where those precious qualities lie.

An auctioneer should have the organ of truth large; of imagination and comparison, considerable; of wit, great; of benevolence, excessively large.

And how happy might such a man be, and cause others to be! He should go through the world laughing, merry, observant, kind-hearted. He should love everything in the world, because his profession regards everything. With books of lighter literature (for I do not recommend the genteel auctioneer to meddle with heavy antiquarian and philological works) he should be elegantly conversant, being able to give a neat history of the author, a pretty sparkling kind criticism of the work, and an appropriate eulogium upon the binding, which would make those people read who never read before; or buy, at least, which is his first consideration. Of pictures we have already spoken. Of china, of jewelry, of gold-headed canes, valuable arms, picturesque antiquities, with what eloquent entrainement might he not speak! He feels every one of these things in his heart. He has all the tastes of the fashionable world. Dr. Meyrick cannot be more enthusiastic about an old suit of armor than he; Sir Harris Nicolas not more eloquent regarding the gallant times in which it was worn, and the brave histories connected with it. He takes up a pearl necklace with as much delight as any beauty who was sighing to wear it round her own snowy throat, and hugs a china monster with as much joy as the oldest duchess could do. Nor must he affect these things; he must feel them. He is a glass in which all the tastes of fashion are reflected. He must be every one of the characters to whom he addresses himself—a genteel Goethe or Shakspeare, a fashionable world-spirit.

How can a man be all this and not be a gentleman; and not have had an education in the midst of the best company—an insight into the most delicate feelings, and wants, and usages? The pulpit oratory of such a man would be invaluable; people would flock to listen to him from far and near. He might out of a single teacup cause streams of world-philosophy to flow, which would be drunk in by grateful thousands; and draw out of an old pincushion points of wit, morals, and experience, that would make a nation wise.

Look round, examine THE ANNALS OF AUCTIONS, as Mr. Robins remarks, and (with every respect for him and his brethren) say, is there in the profession SUCH A MAN? Do we want such a man? Is such a man likely or not likely to make an immense fortune? Can we get such a man except out of the very best society, and among the most favored there?

Everybody answers "No!" I knew you would answer no. And now, gentlemen who have laughed at my pretension to discover a profession, say, have I not? I have laid my finger upon the spot where the social deficit exists. I have shown that we labor under a want; and when the world wants, do we not know that a man will step forth to fill the vacant space that Fate has left for him? Pass we now to the—

SECOND PROFESSION

This profession, too, is a great, lofty and exceptional one, and discovered by me considering these things, and deeply musing upon the necessities of society. Nor let honorable gentlemen imagine that I am enabled to offer them in this profession, more than any other, a promise of what is called future glory, deathless fame, and so forth. All that I say is, that I can put young men in the way of making a comfortable livelihood, and leaving behind them, not a name, but what is better, a decent maintenance to their children. Fitz-Boodle is as good a name as any in England. General Fitz-Boodle, who, in Marlborough's time, and in conjunction with the famous Van Slaap, beat the French in the famous action of Vischzouchee, near Mardyk, in Holland, on the 14th of February, 1709, is promised an immortality upon his tomb in Westminster Abbey; but he died of apoplexy, deucedly in debt, two years afterwards: and what after that is the use of a name?

No, no; the age of chivalry is past. Take the twenty-four first men who come into the club, and ask who they are, and how they made their money? There's Woolsey-Sackville: his father was Lord Chancellor, and sat on the woolsack, whence he took his title; his grandfather dealt in coal-sacks, and not in woolsacks,—small coal-sacks, dribbling out little supplies of black diamonds to the poor. Yonder comes Frank Leveson, in a huge broad-brimmed hat, his shirt-cuffs turned up to his elbows. Leveson is as gentlemanly a fellow as the world contains, and if he has a fault, is perhaps too finikin. Well, you fancy him related to the Sutherland family: nor, indeed, does honest Frank deny it; but entre nous, my good sir, his father was an attorney, and his grandfather a bailiff in Chancery Lane, bearing a name still older than that of Leveson, namely, Levy. So it is that this confounded equality grows and grows, and has laid the good old nobility by the heels. Look at that venerable Sir Charles Kitely, of Kitely Park: he is interested about the Ashantees, and is just come from Exeter Hall. Kitely discounted bills in the City in the year 1787, and gained his baronetcy by a loan to the French princes. All these points of history are perfectly well known; and do you fancy the world cares? Psha! Profession is no disgrace to a man: be what you like, provided you succeed. If Mr. Fauntleroy could come to life with a million of money, you and I would dine with him: you know we would; for why should we be better than our neighbors?

Put, then, out of your head the idea that this or that profession is unworthy of you: take any that may bring you profit, and thank him that puts you in the way of being rich.

The profession I would urge (upon a person duly qualified to undertake it) has, I confess, at the first glance, something ridiculous about it; and will not appear to young ladies so romantic as the calling of a gallant soldier, blazing with glory, gold lace, and vermilion coats; or a dear delightful clergyman, with a sweet blue eye, and a pocket-handkerchief scented charmingly with lavender-water. The profession I allude to WILL, I own, be to young women disagreeable, to sober men trivial, to great stupid moralists unworthy.

But mark my words for it, that in the religious world (I have once or twice, by mistake no doubt, had the honor of dining in "serious" houses, and can vouch for the fact that the dinners there are of excellent quality)—in the serious world, in the great mercantile world, among the legal community (notorious feeders), in every house in town (except some half-dozen which can afford to do without such aid), the man I propose might speedily render himself indispensable.

Does the reader now begin to take? Have I hinted enough for him that he may see with eagle glance the immense beauty of the profession I am about to unfold to him? We have all seen Gunter and Chevet; Fregoso, on the Puerta del Sol (a relation of the ex-Minister Calomarde), is a good purveyor enough for the benighted olla-eaters of Madrid; nor have I any fault to find with Guimard, a Frenchman, who has lately set up in the Toledo, at Naples, where he furnishes people with decent food. It has given me pleasure, too, in walking about London—in the Strand, in Oxford Street, and elsewhere, to see fournisseurs and comestible-merchants newly set up. Messrs. Morel have excellent articles in their warehouses; Fortnum and Mason are known to most of my readers.

But what is not known, what is wanted, what is languished for in England is a DINNER-MASTER,—a gentleman who is not a provider of meat or wine, like the parties before named, who can have no earthly interest in the price of truffled turkeys or dry champagne beyond that legitimate interest which he may feel for his client, and which leads him to see that the latter is not cheated by his tradesmen. For the dinner-giver is almost naturally an ignorant man. How in mercy's name can Mr. Serjeant Snorter, who is all day at Westminster, or in chambers, know possibly the mysteries, the delicacy, of dinner-giving? How can Alderman Pogson know anything beyond the fact that venison is good with currant jelly, and that he likes lots of green fat with his turtle? Snorter knows law, Pogson is acquainted with the state of the tallow-market; but what should he know of eating, like you and me, who have given up our time to it? (I say ME only familiarly, for I have only reached so far in the science as to know that I know nothing.) But men there are, gifted individuals, who have spent years of deep thought—not merely intervals of labor, but hours of study every day—over the gormandizing science,—who, like alchemists, have let their fortunes go, guinea by guinea, into the all-devouring pot,—who, ruined as they sometimes are, never get a guinea by chance but they will have a plate of pease in May with it, or a little feast of ortolans, or a piece of Glo'ster salmon, or one more flask from their favorite claret-bin.

It is not the ruined gastronomist that I would advise a person to select as his TABLE-MASTER; for the opportunities of peculation would be too great in a position of such confidence—such complete abandonment of one man to another. A ruined man would be making bargains with the tradesmen. They would offer to cash bills for him, or send him opportune presents of wine, which he could convert into money, or bribe him in one way or another. Let this be done, and the profession of table-master is ruined. Snorter and Pogson may almost as well order their own dinners, as be at the mercy of a "gastronomic agent" whose faith is not beyond all question.

A vulgar mind, in reply to these remarks regarding the gastronomic ignorance of Snorter and Pogson, might say, "True, these gentlemen know nothing of household economy, being occupied with other more important business elsewhere. But what are their wives about? Lady Pogson in Harley Street has nothing earthly to do but to mind her poodle, and her mantua-maker's and housekeeper's bills. Mrs. Snorter in Belford Place, when she has taken her drive in the Park with the young ladies, may surely have time to attend to her husband's guests and preside over the preparations of his kitchen, as she does worthily at his hospitable mahogany." To this I answer, that a man who expects a woman to understand the philosophy of dinner-giving, shows the strongest evidence of a low mind. He is unjust towards that lovely and delicate creature, woman, to suppose that she heartily understands and cares for what she eats and drinks. No: taken as a rule, women have no real appetites. They are children in the gormandizing way; loving sugar, sops, tarts, trifles, apricot-creams, and such gewgaws. They would take a sip of Malmsey, and would drink currant-wine just as happily, if that accursed liquor were presented to them by the butler. Did you ever know a woman who could lay her fair hand upon her gentle heart and say on her conscience that she preferred dry sillery to sparkling champagne? Such a phenomenon does not exist. They are not made for eating and drinking; or, if they make a pretence to it, become downright odious. Nor can they, I am sure, witness the preparations of a really great repast without a certain jealousy. They grudge spending money (ask guards, coachmen, inn-waiters, whether this be not the case). They will give their all, heaven bless them to serve a son, a grandson, or a dear relative, but they have not the heart to pay for small things magnificently. They are jealous of good dinners, and no wonder. I have shown in a former discourse how they are jealous of smoking, and other personal enjoyments of the male. I say, then, that Lady Pogson or Mrs. Snorter can never conduct their husbands' table properly. Fancy either of them consenting to allow a calf to be stewed down into gravy for one dish, or a dozen hares to be sacrificed to a single puree of game, or the best Madeira to be used for a sauce, or half a dozen of champagne to boil a ham in. They will be for bringing a bottle of Marsala in place of the old particular, or for having the ham cooked in water. But of these matters—of kitchen philosophy—I have no practical or theoretic knowledge; and must beg pardon if, only understanding the goodness of a dish when cooked, I may have unconsciously made some blunder regarding the preparation.

Let it, then, be set down as an axiom, without further trouble of demonstration, that a woman is a bad dinner-caterer; either too great and simple for it, or too mean—I don't know which it is; and gentlemen, according as they admire or contemn the sex, may settle that matter their own way. In brief, the mental constitution of lovely woman is such that she cannot give a great dinner. It must be done by a man. It can't be done by an ordinary man, because he does not understand it. Vain fool! and he sends off to the pastry-cook in Great Russell Street or Baker Street, he lays on a couple of extra waiters (green-grocers in the neighborhood), he makes a great pother with his butler in the cellar, and fancies he has done the business.

Bon Dieu! Who has not been at those dinners?—those monstrous exhibitions of the pastry-cook's art? Who does not know those made dishes with the universal sauce to each: fricandeaux, sweet-breads, damp dumpy cutlets, &c., seasoned with the compound of grease, onions, bad port-wine, cayenne pepper, curry-powder (Warren's blacking, for what I know, but the taste is always the same)—there they lie in the old corner dishes, the poor wiry Moselle and sparkling Burgundy in the ice-coolers, and the old story of white and brown soup, turbot, little smelts, boiled turkey, saddle-of-mutton, and so forth? "Try a little of that fricandeau," says Mrs. Snorter, with a kind smile. "You'll find it, I think, very nice." Be sure it has come in a green tray from Great Russell Street. "Mr. Fitz-Boodle, you have been in Germany," cries Snorter, knowingly; "taste the hock, and tell me what you think of THAT."

How should he know better, poor benighted creature; or she, dear good soul that she is? If they would have a leg-of-mutton and an apple-pudding, and a glass of sherry and port (or simple brandy-and-water called by its own name) after dinner, all would be very well; but they must shine, they must dine as their neighbors. There is no difference in the style of dinners in London; people with five hundred a year treat you exactly as those of five thousand. They WILL have their Moselle or hock, their fatal side-dishes brought in the green trays from the pastry-cook's.

Well, there is no harm done; not as regards the dinner-givers at least, though the dinner-eaters may have to suffer somewhat; it only shows that the former are hospitably inclined, and wish to do the very best in their power,—good honest fellows! If they do wrong, how can they help it? they know no better.

And now, is it not as clear as the sun at noonday, that A WANT exists in London for a superintendent of the table—a gastronomic agent—a dinner-master, as I have called him before? A man of such a profession would be a metropolitan benefit; hundreds of thousands of people of the respectable sort, people in white waistcoats, would thank him daily. Calculate how many dinners are given in the City of London, and calculate the numbers of benedictions that "the Agency" might win.

And as no doubt the observant man of the world has remarked that the freeborn Englishman of the respectable class is, of all others, the most slavish and truckling to a lord; that there is no fly-blown peer but he is pleased to have him at his table, proud beyond measure to call him by his surname (without the lordly prefix); and that those lords whom he does not know, he yet (the freeborn Englishman) takes care to have their pedigrees and ages by heart from his world-bible, the "Peerage:" as this is an indisputable fact, and as it is in this particular class of Britons that our agent must look to find clients, I need not say it is necessary that the agent should be as high-born as possible, and that he should be able to tack, if possible, an honorable or some other handle to his respectable name. He must have it on his professional card—

THE HONORABLE GEORGE GORMAND GOBBLETON,

Apician Chambers, Pall Mall.

Or,

SIR AUGUSTUS CARVER CRAMLEY CRAMLEY,

Amphitryonic Council Office, Swallow Street.

or, in some such neat way, Gothic letters on a large handsome crockeryware card, with possibly a gilt coat-of-arms and supporters, or the blood-red hand of baronetcy duly displayed. Depend on it plenty of guineas will fall in it, and that Gobbleton's supporters will support him comfortably enough.

For this profession is not like that of the auctioneer, which I take to be a far more noble one, because more varied and more truthful; but in the Agency case, a little humbug at least is necessary. A man cannot be a successful agent by the mere force of his simple merit or genius in eating and drinking. He must of necessity impose upon the vulgar to a certain degree. He must be of that rank which will lead them naturally to respect him, otherwise they might be led to jeer at his profession; but let a noble exercise it, and bless your soul, all the "Court Guide" is dumb!

He will then give out in a manly and somewhat pompous address what has before been mentioned, namely, that he has seen the fatal way in which the hospitality of England has been perverted hitherto, accapare'd by a few cooks with green trays. (He must use a good deal of French in his language, for that is considered very gentlemanlike by vulgar people.) He will take a set of chambers in Canton Gardens, which will be richly though severely furnished, and the door of which will be opened by a French valet (he MUST be a Frenchman, remember), who will say, on letting Mr. Snorter or Sir Benjamin Pogson in, that "MILOR is at home." Pogson will then be shown into a library furnished with massive bookcases, containing all the works on cookery and wines (the titles of them) in all the known languages in the world. Any books, of course, will do, as you will have them handsomely bound, and keep them under plate-glass. On a side-table will be little sample-bottles of wine, a few truffles on a white porcelain saucer, a prodigious strawberry or two, perhaps, at the time when such fruit costs much money. On the library will be busts marked Ude, Careme, Bechamel, in marble (never mind what heads, of course); and, perhaps, on the clock should be a figure of the Prince of Conde's cook killing himself because the fish had not arrived in time: there may be a wreath of immortelles on the figure to give it a more decidedly Frenchified air. The walls will be of a dark rich paper, hung round with neat gilt frames, containing plans of menus of various great dinners, those of Cambaceres, Napoleon, Louis XIV., Louis XVIII., Heliogabalus if you like, each signed by the respective cook.

After the stranger has looked about him at these things, which he does not understand in the least, especially the truffles, which look like dirty potatoes, you will make your appearance, dressed in a dark dress, with one handsome enormous gold chain, and one large diamond ring; a gold snuff-box, of course, which you will thrust into the visitor's paw before saying a word. You will be yourself a portly grave man, with your hair a little bald and gray. In fact, in this, as in all other professions, you had best try to look as like Canning as you can.

When Pogson has done sneezing with the snuff, you will say to him, "Take a fauteuil. I have the honor of addressing Sir Benjamin Pogson, I believe?" And then you will explain to him your system.

This, of course, must vary with every person you address. But let us lay down a few of the heads of a plan which may be useful, or may be modified infinitely, or may be cast aside altogether, just as circumstances dictate. After all I am not going to turn gastronomic agent, and speak only for the benefit perhaps of the very person who is reading this:—

"SYNOPSIS OF THE GASTRONOMIC AGENCY OF THE HONORABLE GEORGE GOBBLETON.

"The Gastronomic Agent having traversed Europe, and dined with the best society of the world, has been led naturally, as a patriot, to turn his thoughts homeward, and cannot but deplore the lamentable ignorance regarding gastronomy displayed in a country for which Nature has done almost everything.

"But it is ever singularly thus. Inherent ignorance belongs to man; and The Agent, in his Continental travels, has always remarked, that the countries most fertile in themselves were invariably worse tilled than those more barren. The Italians and the Spaniards leave their fields to Nature, as we leave our vegetables, fish, and meat. And, heavens! what richness do we fling away, what dormant qualities in our dishes do we disregard,—what glorious gastronomic crops (if the Agent may be permitted the expression)—what glorious gastronomic crops do we sacrifice, allowing our goodly meats and fishes to lie fallow! 'Chance,' it is said by an ingenious historian, who, having been long a secretary in the East India House, must certainly have had access to the best information upon Eastern matters—'Chance,' it is said by Mr. Charles Lamb, 'which burnt down a Chinaman's house, with a litter of sucking-pigs that were unable to escape from the interior, discovered to the world the excellence of roast-pig.' Gunpowder, we know, was invented by a similar fortuity." [The reader will observe that my style in the supposed character of a Gastronomic Agent is purposely pompous and loud.] "So, 'tis said, was printing,—so glass.—We should have drunk our wine poisoned with the villanous odor of the borachio, had not some Eastern merchants, lighting their fires in the Desert, marked the strange composition which now glitters on our sideboards, and holds the costly produce of our vines.

"We have spoken of the natural riches of a country. Let the reader think but for one moment of the gastronomic wealth of our country of England, and he will be lost in thankful amazement as he watches the astonishing riches poured out upon us from Nature's bounteous cornucopia! Look at our fisheries!— the trout and salmon tossing in our brawling streams; the white and full-breasted turbot struggling in the mariner's net; the purple lobster lured by hopes of greed into his basket-prison, which he quits only for the red ordeal of the pot. Look at whitebait, great heavens!—look at whitebait, and a thousand frisking, glittering, silvery things besides, which the nymphs of our native streams bear kindly to the deities of our kitchens—our kitchens such as they are.

"And though it may be said that other countries produce the freckle-backed salmon and the dark broad-shouldered turbot; though trout frequent many a stream besides those of England, and lobsters sprawl on other sands than ours; yet, let it be remembered, that our native country possesses these altogether, while other lands only know them separately; that, above all, whitebait is peculiarly our country's—our city's own! Blessings and eternal praises be on it, and, of course, on brown bread and butter! And the Briton should further remember, with honest pride and thankfulness, the situation of his capital, of London: the lordly turtle floats from the sea into the stream, and from the stream to the city; the rapid fleets of all the world se donnent rendezvous in the docks of our silvery Thames; the produce of our coasts and provincial cities, east and west, is borne to us on the swift lines of lightning railroads. In a word—and no man but one who, like The Agent, has travelled Europe over, can appreciate the gift—there is no city on earth's surface so well supplied with fish as London!

"With respect to our meats, all praise is supererogatory. Ask the wretched hunter of chevreuil, the poor devourer of rehbraten, what they think of the noble English haunch, that, after bounding in the Park of Knole or Windsor, exposes its magnificent flank upon some broad silver platter at our tables? It is enough to say of foreign venison, that THEY ARE OBLIGED TO LARD IT. Away! ours is the palm of roast; whether of the crisp mutton that crops the thymy herbage of our downs, or the noble ox who revels on lush Althorpian oil-cakes. What game is like to ours? Mans excels us in poultry, 'tis true; but 'tis only in merry England that the partridge has a flavor, that the turkey can almost se passer de truffes, that the jolly juicy goose can be eaten as he deserves.

"Our vegetables, moreover, surpass all comment; Art (by the means of glass) has wrung fruit out of the bosom of Nature, such as she grants to no other clime. And if we have no vineyards on our hills, we have gold to purchase their best produce. Nature, and enterprise that masters Nature, have done everything for our land.

"But, with all these prodigious riches in our power, is it not painful to reflect how absurdly we employ them? Can we say that we are in the habit of dining well? Alas, no! and The Agent, roaming o'er foreign lands, and seeing how, with small means and great ingenuity and perseverance, great ends were effected, comes back sadly to his own country, whose wealth he sees absurdly wasted, whose energies are misdirected, and whose vast capabilities are allowed to lie idle. . . ." [Here should follow what I have only hinted at previously, a vivid and terrible picture of the degradation of our table.] ". . . Oh, for a master spirit, to give an impetus to the land, to see its great power directed in the right way, and its wealth not squandered or hidden, but nobly put out to interest and spent!

"The Agent dares not hope to win that proud station—to be the destroyer of a barbarous system wallowing in abusive prodigality—to become a dietetic reformer—the Luther of the table.

"But convinced of the wrongs which exist, he will do his humble endeavor to set them right, and to those who know that they are ignorant (and this is a vast step to knowledge) he offers his counsels, his active co-operation, his frank and kindly sympathy. The Agent's qualifications are these:— '1. He is of one of the best families in England; and has in himself, or through his ancestors, been accustomed to good living for centuries. In the reign of Henry V., his maternal great-great-grandfather, Roger de

Gobylton' [the name may be varied, of course, or the king's reign, or the dish invented], 'was the first who discovered the method of roasting a peacock whole, with his tail-feathers displayed; and the dish was served to the two kings at Rouen. Sir Walter Cramley, in Elizabeth's reign, produced before her Majesty, when at Killingworth Castle, mackerel with the famous GOOSEBERRY SAUCE, &c.'

"2. He has, through life, devoted himself to no other study than that of the table: and has visited to that end the courts of all the monarchs of Europe: taking the receipts of the cooks, with whom he lives on terms of intimate friendship, often at enormous expense to himself.

"3. He has the same acquaintance with all the vintages of the Continent; having passed the autumn of 1811 (the comet year) on the great Weinberg of Johannisberg; being employed similarly at Bordeaux, in 1834; at Oporto, in 1820; and at Xeres de la Frontera, with his excellent friends, Duff, Gordon and Co., the year after. He travelled to India and back in company with fourteen pipes of Madeira (on board of the Samuel Snob' East Indiaman, Captain Scuttler), and spent the vintage season in the island, with unlimited powers of observation granted to him by the great houses there.

"4. He has attended Mr. Groves of Charing Cross, and Mr. Giblett of Bond Street, in a course of purchases of fish and meat; and is able at a glance to recognize the age of mutton, the primeness of beef, the firmness and freshness of fish of all kinds.

"5. He has visited the parks, the grouse-manors, and the principal gardens of England, in a similar professional point of view."

The Agent then, through his subordinates, engages to provide gentlemen who are about to give dinner-parties—"1. With cooks to dress the dinners; a list of which gentlemen he has by him, and will recommend none who are not worthy of the strictest confidence.

"2. With a menu for the table, according to the price which the Amphitryon chooses to incur.

"3. He will, through correspondence, with the various fournisseurs of the metropolis, provide them with viands, fruit, wine, &c., sending to Paris, if need be, where he has a regular correspondence with Messrs. Chevet.

"4. He has a list of dexterous table-waiters (all answering to the name of John for fear of mistakes, the butler's name to be settled according to pleasure), and would strongly recommend that the servants of the house should be locked in the back-kitchen or servants' hall during the time the dinner takes place.

"5. He will receive and examine all the accounts of the fournisseurs,—of course pledging his honor as a gentleman not to receive one shilling of paltry gratification from the tradesmen he employs, but to see that the bills are more moderate, and their goods of better quality, than they would provide to any person of less experience than himself.

"6. His fee for superintending a dinner will be five guineas: and The Agent entreats his clients to trust ENTIRELY to him and his subordinates for the arrangement of the repast,—NOT TO THINK of inserting dishes of their own invention, or producing wine from their own cellars, as he engages to have it brought in the best order, and fit for immediate drinking. Should the Amphitryon, however, desire some particular dish or wine, he must consult The Agent in the first case by writing, in the second, by sending a sample to The Agent's chambers. For it is manifest that the whole complexion of a dinner may be altered by the insertion of a single dish; and, therefore, parties will do well to mention their wishes on the first interview with The Agent. He cannot be called upon to recompose his bill of fare, except at great risk to the ensemble of the dinner and enormous inconvenience to himself.

"7. The Agent will be at home for consultation from ten o'clock until two, earlier if gentlemen who are engaged at early hours in the City desire to have an interview: and be it remembered, that a PERSONAL INTERVIEW is always the best: for it is greatly necessary to know not only the number but the character of the guests whom the Amphitryon proposes to entertain,—whether they are fond of any particular wine or dish, what is their state of health, rank, style, profession, &c.

"8. At two o'clock, he will commence his rounds; for as the metropolis is wide, it is clear that he must be early in the field in some districts. From 2 to 3 he will be in Russell Square and the neighborhood; 3 to 3 3/4, Harley Street, Portland Place, Cavendish Square, and the environs; 3 3/4 to 4 1/4, Portman Square, Gloucester Place, Baker Street, &c.; 4 1/4 to 5, the new district about Hyde Park Terrace; 5 to 5 3/4, St. John's Wood and the Regent's Park. He will be in Grosvenor Square by 6, and in Belgrave Square, Pimlico, and its vicinity, by 7. Parties there are requested not to dine until 8 o'clock; and The Agent, once for all, peremptorily announces that he will NOT go to the palace, where it is utterly impossible to serve a good dinner."

"TO TRADESMEN.

"Every Monday evening during the season the Gastronomic Agent proposes to give a series of trial-dinners, to which the principal gormands of the metropolis, and a few of The Agent's most respectable clients, will be invited. Covers will be laid for TEN at nine o'clock precisely. And as The Agent does not propose to exact a single shilling of profit from their bills, and as his recommendation will be of infinite value to them, the tradesmen he employs will furnish the weekly dinner gratis. Cooks will attend (who have acknowledged characters) upon the same terms. To save trouble, a book will be kept where butchers, poulterers, fishmongers, &c. may inscribe their names in order, taking it by turns to supply the trial-table. Wine-merchants will naturally compete every week promiscuously, sending what they consider their best samples, and leaving with the hall-porter tickets of the prices. Confectionery to be done out of the house. Fruiterers, market-men, as butchers and poulterers. The Agent's maitre-d'hotel will give a receipt to each individual for the articles he produces; and let all remember that The Agent is a VERY KEEN JUDGE, and woe betide those who serve him or his clients ill!

"GEORGE GORMAND GOBBLETON.

"CARLTON GARDENS, June 10, 1842."

Here I have sketched out the heads of such an address as I conceive a gastronomic agent might put forth; and appeal pretty confidently to the British public regarding its merits and my own discovery. If this be not a profession—a new one—a feasible one—a lucrative one,—I don't know what is. Say that a man attends but fifteen dinners daily, that is seventy-five guineas, or five hundred and fifty pounds weekly, or fourteen thousand three hundred pounds for a season of six months: and how many of our younger sons have such a capital even? Let, then, some unemployed gentleman with the requisite qualifications come forward. It will not be necessary that he should have done all that is stated in the prospectus; but, at any rate, let him SAY he has: there can't be much harm in an innocent fib of that sort; for the gastronomic agent must be a sort of dinner-pope, whose opinions cannot be supposed to err.

And as he really will be an excellent judge of eating and drinking, and will bring his whole mind to bear upon the question, and will speedily acquire an experience which no person out of the profession can possibly have; and as, moreover, he will be an honorable man, not practising upon his client in any way, or demanding sixpence beyond his just fee, the world will gain vastly by the coming forward of such a person,—gain in good dinners, and absolutely save money: for what is five guineas for a dinner of sixteen? The sum may be gaspille by a cook-wench, or by one of those abominable before-named pastry-cooks with their green trays.

If any man take up the business, he will invite me, of course, to the Monday dinners. Or does ingratitude go so far as that a man should forget the author of his good fortune? I believe it does. Turn we away from the sickening theme!

And now, having concluded my professions, how shall I express my obligations to the discriminating press of this country for the unanimous applause which hailed my first appearance? It is the more wonderful, as I pledge my sacred word, I never wrote a document before much longer than a laundress's bill, or the acceptance of an invitation to dinner. But enough of this egotism: thanks for praise conferred sound like vanity; gratitude is hard to speak of, and at present it swells the full heart of

GEORGE SAVAGE FITZ-BOODLE.

William Makepeace Thackeray – A Short Biography

William Makepeace Thackeray, was born on July 18th, 1811 in Calcutta, then British India, where his father, Richmond Thackeray was the secretary to the Board of Revenue in the British East India Company. His mother, Anne Becher also worked for the British East India Company.

His father died in 1815, and his mother sent Thackeray to England the following year while she remained in India and would, sometime later, marry her childhood sweetheart. En-route to England the ship stopped for provisions on St. Helena. The Imprisoned Napoleon was pointed out to him by a servant with the words that he "eats three sheep every day, and all the little children he can lay hands on!"

Finally, back in England the young Thackeray was sent to school, initially in Southampton and Chiswick, before being moved to Charterhouse School. Charterhouse and Thackeray did not take to each other but the time became a valuable source for his later work "Slaughterhouse". Despite his less than respectful recalling of his time with them Charterhouse placed a monument in the chapel after his death.

In his final year at Charterhouse a troubling illness delayed his departure to attend Cambridge University. Over the course of his life Thackeray would suffer from ill health, much of it brought about for his fondness for "gluttling and gorging". Excess was something he could enjoy and for a man who stood some 6' 3" it would appear to the eye that, initially at least, his large frame could absorb much of that excess.

However, Thackeray's lazy attitude to completely mastering anything he set his mind too, especially where ambition for academia was involved, meant he departed Cambridge little more than a year after joining. He had however published two short works in University periodicals. As an author, he would have quite some impact on English literature in the years to come, so it seems difficult to reconcile that he felt no urgency to pursue writing at that time.

He now spent some time travelling across Europe stopping at both Paris, to study art, and to winter in Weimar. Back in London a final attempt was made on a professional career. This time studying law at Middle Temple. It lasted no more than a few months.

Now, having reached 21, he received his father's inheritance. It was a very substantial estate of 17,000 pounds, an enormous sum of money at the time. However, although Thackeray had youth he lacked a little in energy and certainly much financial experience. He funded not one but two newspapers, and neither was to prove successful. Gambling seemed enjoyable and certainly he had money to lose, which he did on a regular basis. Further investments in two soon-to-fail Indian banks quickly ensured little of his good fortune remained.

He now had to consider taking up yet another profession. Thackeray turned to art hoping that his studies in Paris would prove of benefit. Unfortunately, they did not. His ambivalent attitude continued until on August 20th, 1836 he married the 20-year-old, Isabella Gethin Shawe. It seemed to prove a turning point in many ways.

The marriage would produce three daughters; Anne Isabella in 1837, Jane, in 1838, who tragically died in infancy and Harriet Marian in 1840.

Now, as a husband and father, Thackeray seemed at last to understand his responsibilities to nurture and provide.

His early efforts at "writing for his life" were to establish his career as a foremost author. His main employment was with Fraser's Magazine, a sharp-witted and sharp-tongued conservative publication for which he produced art criticism, short fictional sketches, and who would also serialise two of his novels. He also found time, between 1837 and 1840 to review books for The Times and to make regular contributions to The Morning Chronicle and The Foreign Quarterly Review.

In his earliest works, which he wrote under various pseudonyms including; Charles James Yellowplush, Michael Angelo Titmarsh and George Savage Fitz-Boodle, he tended towards savagery in his attacks on high society, military prowess, the institution of marriage and hypocrisy.

Between May 1839 and February 1840 Fraser's published Catherine. Originally intended as a satire of the Newgate school of crime fiction, it ended up being more of a picaresque tale. Thackeray also began work on what would eventually become A Shabby Genteel Story.

However, Thackeray, having successfully found a career that he cared about and had the talent for, found that his personal life was about to descend into chaos. After the birth of her third child in 1840, Isabella, sank into depression. At first Thackeray, didn't think too much of it. He needed to work to earn an income to support his family and finding that Isabella was distracting both herself and him he realised he could get no work done at home and so spent more and more time away until finally, in September 1840, it dawned upon him how serious his wife's condition had become. Struck by guilt, he set out with his wife to Ireland. During the boat crossing she threw herself into the sea, but was thankfully pulled from the waters. Her mother who had little understanding of her daughter's illness was of little help and perhaps a hinderance. After four-weeks they returned to England. From November 1840 to February 1842 Isabella was in and out of professional care, as her condition waxed and waned.

Isabella eventually deteriorated into a permanent state of detachment. Thackeray desperately sought cures for her, but nothing worked, and she ended up in two different asylums in or near Paris until 1845, after which Thackeray took her back to England, where he installed her with a Mrs Bakewell at Camberwell. Despite her condition Isabella would outlive her husband by 3 decades.

After his wife's illness Thackeray became a de facto widower, never able to establish another permanent relationship.

In 1843, through his connection to the illustrator John Leech, whom he had met at Charterhouse, he began writing for the newly created magazine Punch, in which he published The Snob Papers, later collected as The Book of Snobs. Thackeray was a regular contributor to Punch until 1854.

Thackeray had earlier received some success with two travel books, The Paris Sketch Book and The Irish Sketch Book, the latter marked by hostility to Irish Catholics. The book appealed to British prejudices, and on that basis Thackeray now became Punch's Irish expert, often under the pseudonym Hibernis Hibernior. It was Thackeray's writings that were the basis for Punch's notoriously harsh, hostile and condescending depictions of the Irish during the devastating Irish Famine (1845–51).

As well as his regular columns and contributions Thackeray worked on his novels. In The Luck of Barry Lyndon, which was serialised in Fraser's in 1844, he explored the situation of an outsider trying to achieve status in high society, a theme he developed more successfully a few years later with Vanity Fair.

Thackeray achieved more recognition with his Snob Papers (serialised 1846/7, and published as a book in 1848), but the work that really established his fame was the novel Vanity Fair, which first appeared in serialised instalments beginning in January 1847.

Published as a book the novel had a slow start but eventually sales rose to 7,000 copies a month. Just as importantly, it was the book that everybody was talking about. Thackeray finally had a name that gained notice and was reviewed in journals such as the famed, and much sought after, Edinburgh Review.

The accolades and success also gave him a respite from writing everything in a manner that would help ensure income rather than literary respect. Even before Vanity Fair completed its serial run Thackeray had become a celebrity, sought after by the very lords and ladies whom he satirised. with the character of Becky Sharp, the artist's daughter who rises high by manipulating all around her.

Pendennis followed in 1849-50, but it was interrupted halfway through writing for 3 months by a severe illness. Some accounts say it was cholera. Pendennis is a semi-autobiographical bildungsroman that draws on, among other things, Thackeray's disappointments in college, his ambivalent relationship with his mother, and his insider's knowledge of the London publishing world.

This novel ran at the same time as Charles Dicken's David Copperfield, and their dual appearance brought about the first of many comparisons with Dickens. Thackeray, for his part, felt that he and

Dickens were battling for supremacy, though he would never equal Dickens's popularity, except with the critics.

Interestingly the two were involved in a spat which became known as the "Garrick Club affair". Thackeray and Dickens had skirmished over the "Dignity of Literature" and had other slight disagreements but this literary quarrel caused a rift in their friendship that lasted almost until the end of Thackeray's life. The relationship was healed only in Thackeray's last months, through a surprise meeting and handshake on the steps of a London club. Thackeray had taken offense at some personal remarks in a column by Edmund Yates and demanded an apology, eventually taking the affair to the Garrick Club committee. Already upset with Thackeray for an indiscreet remark about his affair with Ellen Ternan, Dickens championed Yates, helping him to write letters both to Thackeray and, in his defense, to the club's committee. Despite the intervention of Dickens, Yates eventually lost the vote of the Club's members, but the quarrel was laid out for the public in journal articles and pamphlets. "What pains me most," Thackeray said at the time, "is that Dickens should have been his adviser, and next that I should have had to lay a heavy hand on a young man who, I take it, has been cruelly punished by the issue of the affair, and I believe is hardly aware of the nature of his own offence, and doesn't even now understand that a gentleman should resent the monstrous insult which he volunteered".

Aside from these quarrelsome, distracting literary disagreements and Isabella's on-going illness life was good for Thackeray. He was to remain as he put it "at the top of the tree," for the rest of his life. The works for which he is so well remembered; Vanity Fair and Barry Lyndon had established that but he continued to write and produce novels, stories, sketches and works profusely.

To remain at such a high level in both quality and quantity is somewhat surprising given the continuation and escalation of various illnesses which continued to haunt him.

With Isabella still unwell Thackeray did seek out other women, in particular Mrs Jane Brookfield. Despite his hopes, it always felt that he was pursuing her as she battled the problems of her own marriage and turned to Thackeray for comfort and support. A source for these relationships often came on the lecture tours of Great Britain and the United States which he now entertained. These tours gave the public a chance to see and hear their hero's and provided another valuable source of income for those invited to tour. Whilst in in New York he met the Baxter family. Sally, the eldest daughter, enchanted the novelist—as a number of vibrant, intelligent, beautiful young women had done before her—and she became the model for Ethel Newcome. He visited her on his second tour of the States when she was married to a South Carolina gentleman. His choosing of married women in the shape of both Jane and Sally was ill-advised and both relationships led nowhere but did take quite some time to disassemble and for reason to set in.

In 1852, The History of Henry Esmond was published as a 3-volume novel without first being serialised and in a special type meant to imitate the appearance of an eighteenth-century book. This was the most carefully planned of Thackeray's novels. The book was celebrated for its brilliance, and Thackeray recognized it as "the very best I can do". At the time, it caused a sensation thanks to its controversial ending, wherein the hero marries a woman who early in the novel seemed more like a "mother" to him.

The eighteenth-century held a great attraction for Thackeray and he had previously set both Barry Lyndon and Catherine there as well as the sequel to Esmond, The Virginians, which takes place in North America and includes George Washington as a character.

Thackeray had twice visited the United States on lecture tours during this period as well as given lectures in London on the English humorists of the eighteenth century, and on the first four Hanoverian monarchs. The latter were published in a book as The Four Georges.

Interestingly Thackeray also decided that Politics was something he could more than dabble in. In Oxford he stood as an independent for Parliament. He was narrowly beaten by Cardwell, a politician who was substituted for the man Thackeray thought he was going to run against, although Thackeray's advocacy of entertainment on the Sabbath would have done little to help his campaign. Even so the margin of his defeat was only 1,070 votes, to Thackeray's 1,005.

In 1860 Thackeray became editor of the newly established Cornhill Magazine, a role he never felt truly comfortable in, preferring to contribute as a columnist on the Roundabout Papers. However, the financial compensation was by all accounts quite extraordinary. The Cornhill began its history with a record circulation and a number of distinguished contributors swayed onboard by Thackeray's reputation. It was in the Cornhill that he serialised his last complete novel, The Adventures of Philip in 1861-62. (After his death, the incomplete Denis Duval would also appear there in 1864).

After two years as editor he stepped down, primarily to concentrate on writing novels again. A piece he wrote for the Cornhill at this time "Thorns in the Cushion," one of The Roundabout Papers, fondly assembles the pains he felt in rejecting manuscripts on the one hand and receiving criticism of the magazine on the other. It seemed a good time to move on.

Thackeray's health had worsened during the 1850s and he was plagued by a recurring stricture of the urethra that laid him up for days at a time. He also felt that he had lost much of his creative impetus. He worsened matters by excessively eating and drinking, and avoiding exercise, though he enjoyed horseback-riding. He has been described as "the greatest literary glutton who ever lived". Indeed, his main activity apart from writing was eating and drinking and many of his stories include elaborate scenes and themes on his fondness for them.

On December 23rd, 1863, William Makepeace Thackeray, after returning from dining out and before dressing for bed, suffered a massive stroke. He was found dead on his bed the following morning. He was only fifty-two.

His death was entirely unexpected, and shocked family, friends and indeed the entire Nation.

It is said that at his funeral service thousands of mourners turned out to witness his passing. He was buried on December 29th at Kensal Green Cemetery, London.

William Makepeace Thackeray – A Concise Bibliography

The Yellowplush Papers (1837)
Catherine (1839–40)
A Shabby Genteel Story (1840)
Second Funeral of Napoleon (1841)
The Irish Sketchbook (1843)
The Luck of Barry Lyndon (1844)

Notes of a Journey from Cornhill to Grand Cairo (1846)
Mrs. Perkins's Ball (1846), under the name M. A. Titmarsh
Stray Papers: Being Stories, Reviews, Verses, and Sketches (1821-1847)
The Book of Snobs (1848)
Vanity Fair (1848)
Pendennis (1848–1850)
Rebecca and Rowena (1850)
The Paris Sketchbook (1840)
Men's Wives (1852)
The History of Henry Esmond (1852)
The English Humorists of the Eighteenth Century (1853)
The Newcomes (1855)
The Rose and the Ring (1855)
The Virginians (1857–1859)
Lovel the Widower (1860)
Four Georges (1860-1861)
The Adventures of Philip (1862)
Roundabout Papers (1863)
Denis Duval (1864)
The English Humorists of the eighteenth century: A Series of Six Lectures (1867)
Ballads (1869)
Burlesques (1869)
The Orphan of Pimlico (1876)

Thackeray wrote a numerous number of articles for magazines and the like as well as contributing many picture sketches to articles and his own books. Many were then collected and published together. We have listed his major works only for this bibliography.

www.ingramcontent.com/pod-product-compliance
Lightning Source LLC
Chambersburg PA
CBHW061458170626
46811CB00004B/1565